The Girl in the House

A PSYCHOLOGICAL THRILLER

HARSHVARDHAN RAO

Srishti
Publishers & Distributors

Srishti Publishers & Distributors
A unit of AJR Publishing LLP
212A, Peacock Lane
Shahpur Jat, New Delhi – 110 049

editorial@srishtipublishers.com

First published by
Srishti Publishers & Distributors in 2023

10 9 8 7 6 5 4 3 2 1

Printed and bound in India

To my wife Megha,
and my children Vihaan and Rishvik.

1
The Address

A few boys were standing behind the concrete fence, looking at the lawn of Villa no 666/13B. Six pairs of adolescent eyes, scanning the yard to spot their cricket ball.

All of a sudden, one of the boys pointed in one direction and shouted, “It’s there! See, it’s there! Near that bush beside the staircase.”

Everyone beamed their eyes at that spot and shouted in unison, “Yes, yes! It’s there.”

Now the task of bringing the ball back silenced that little celebration of discovering the ball. They all went quiet, and everyone turned their head to one boy in the group.

Someone said looking at him, “Now you go and bring it.”

He started to sweat profusely. The adolescent face was terrified by the task of bringing the ball. Frightened, the boy replied in a crying voice.

“I will not bring it. You go and bring it.”

The pressure of losing the ball to one of the most haunted houses in the city was much higher than anything else. Suddenly, the hustle started to push and nudge each other in the effort that someone in the group would bring the ball back. One voice came out from the group.

“We all have one rule which we have to follow; whoever hits the ball inside the house will have to bring it back.”

"I am not going in there; that witch will kill me. My sister says witches like small boys."

Another boy insisted, "Your sister is making a fool out of you. Go, nothing will happen, bring the ball." The request and insistence bordered on bullying him into bringing it back.

After a lot of convincing and arguments, one boy agreed to get the ball back. He jumped the fence and went in. He briskly walked across the lawn, reached the stairs while keeping his eyes on the ground. He swiftly went near the bush and picked the ball with his left hand. All of a sudden, the sound of the window slowly opening was heard. The boy was terrified. He tried hard not to look at the window, but was unable to stop himself from glancing back while walking away. He saw a girl appear from the dark in the house, as if she was floating in the air. She stopped near the window. The boy looked at her and stood rooted to the spot. His heart began to pound. She didn't look normal in any way, with her untidy long black hair, a shiny pair of eyes, and an eye socket that was visible. She was a thin and bony figure, with blood stains on her arms, wearing a long white dress. Her face was white, with light blue patches here and there, and she stared back at him. After few seconds, she started to rise in the air. The girl looked at the boy and gave a ghostly smile.

It sent a chill down his spine. He shrieked, "Mummy! Mummy! Ghost!" and ran towards the fence holding his breath. While running blindly towards the wall, he stumbled on a stone. He got up swiftly, without looking at his leg. Blood had started to gush from his knee. The other boys gave him a hand.

The boy tried to get up, but his whole body shook and shivered. As he tried to get up, he felt a sharp spike of pain. The pain increased with each step, and he felt as if someone was trying to pull him inside the house.

The sound of a loud bang in the house fuelled fear among the boys. It was the sound of the flap of the window where the girl stood. Hearing the sound, everyone screamed.

"Run! Run!"

The boy used all the strength he had and finally managed to grab someone's hand. All of them quickly pulled him up. After a few seconds, the ground was empty. There was no sign that anyone had been playing near the house.

Villa 666/13B had a new story added – that of a ghost in the house.

But the question remained unanswered. Whose ghost was inside the house?

2
G.B. Studio

The G.B. studio had been so quiet since morning that Ratan had started to doze off just before noon. The only thing keeping him awake was the buzzing of the electric racket when the houseflies stuck to it. Ravi was busy counting the houseflies he had killed so far.

"You know Ratan, no matter how many times you shoo these flies away from our shop, they always come back. So you don't have any option but to kill them," he chuckled as there was another sound of a fly sticking to the racket.

"I disagree with that logic as I have told you many times. I remember reading about the Buddhist way of pest control to get rid of pests, where you don't have to kill them," Ratan replied.

"Are you serious? You want me to chant mantras to remove these flies," Ravi giggled and continued. "Let me tell you something. I have one secret mantra," he extended his hand below the cabinet, picked up the insect spray, pointed the nozzle at the window and pressed it. Ravi looked at Ratan and said, "This is my new mantra, Mr. Ratan Gandhi."

Ratan waved his hand in disagreement, kept his head on the wall, and started to doze off again.

G.B. studio was a setup built together by two childhood friends Jignesh Gandhi and Moolchand Bhagat, in the late 80s. The name 'Gandhi and Bhagat' gave the shop a deep air of patriotism. They had grown up together and also met their destiny together in a bus accident while returning from a visit to a shrine. After that unfortunate incident, Jignesh's son Ratan and Moolchand's son Ravi were the successors of the shop. The G.B. studio was a famous name in town, so it was easy to run business. Ratan and Ravi were never intelligent kids; they had dropped out of college, showing a lack of interest in their studies. When Jignesh and Moolchand were alive, they didn't have any hopes from their sons. Ratan and Ravi were of the same age – in their late twenties, fair and tall, and welcomed anyone who walked into the shop with a warm smile.

Due to digitalization, customers at the G.B. studio had declined. The shop mostly made money when there were exams as many customers would come to get their photos taken for their admit cards. Ratan and Ravi were neither good businessmen nor good photographers, so the business was as good as their talent.

Recently they had renovated the interiors of the shop and also bought some new equipment for the camera. It was with the belief that this new look would add more glamour to the shop and therefore attract more customers. But unfortunately, it hadn't worked out. To make things worse, they had taken a loan from a loan shark.

That evening Ravi closed the shop, and both were returning home. Business was almost dry. There had been no income since the last couple of days and it was quite evident on their faces.

While walking down the parking, Ravi kept his hand on Ratan's shoulder, took a deep breath, and said, "I don't think we will ever make our fathers proud. We are neither good photographers nor good businessmen. Shall we sell the shop and start some other business?"

"Like what?" Ratan asked curiously.

"I haven't given it detailed thought, but how about a grocery store?" Ravi replied and turned towards the scooter stand nearby.

Ratan, following him, said, "From where do you get these ideas? Stick to the shop and work hard; we will find some way out to make it work."

"Don't tell me to chant any mantras, please," Ravi grinned and took out the scooter from the parking.

"You must try some yoga and meditation, Ravi. This will help you to get rid of these crazy ideas," Ratan said and hopped on the scooter behind Ravi.

While going back, it was almost a ritual for them to stop at the stall near their house to eat some snacks. The time at the stall gave them a break from the frustrating, unproductive day spent at the shop and lightened their mood.

Saleem uncle, short with grey hair, was a good friend of Ravi and Ratan's fathers. In his late 50s, he was the owner and chef of a tiny shop that sold snacks from evening till late into the night. The shop which was located near the city garden was usually crowded till late night. There was ample open space in front of the shop, the part which curved out of the garden area, where people liked to sit and spend most of the time chitchatting. Lately, the shop had become famous for the pav bhaji it served. Saleem had some secret spices, which he mixed with the bhaji to make it tempting and mouthwatering. When asked what it was, the soft-spoken Saleem said, "Nothing but love!"

Ratan and Ravi reached the shop and found one empty table.

"I hope you remember we have to pay for the new setup in the studio. How are we going to pay this month's installment?" Ratan asked worried.

"I am telling you to sell this shop," Ravi said.

"Can you come out of that loop, please? And think about this month's installment. How we are going to pay..." Ratan replied with frustration.

"Take some money from me. Pay me later once you have it," Saleem uncle said, handing over the plate of pav bhaji to them.

"Thank you, uncle. We can't take it from you. You have helped us a lot in the past. We will work hard and earn it. Don't worry," Ratan said.

"Take it, Ratan. I insist," Saleem uncle said, looking at Ravi, who was busy digging into the pav bhaji.

Saleem knew that Ravi had no hope left in the shop making any money. On the other hand, Ratan was eager to run the business. But that disagreement between them was not enough to break Ratan and Ravi's friendship. They supported each other's decisions, and this uniqueness in their friendship had always charmed Saleem uncle. It reminded Saleem of their fathers' friendship.

"During your fathers' time, things were different. The camera was new. Shooting photos at every event was what people wanted. It was a trend to hire photographers for even a simple birthday party. Now the world has changed a lot. Saleem took out a smartphone from his pocket and said, "See, Saleem studio!" he chuckled and continued, "Why don't you try to reach out to newspapers, magazines? They also need a photographer for their daily job. Isn't it?"

"It's not that easy, uncle," Ravi kept the pav bhaji plate on the table and gulped down a glass of water.

"Nothing is easy, my son. Even that pav bhaji you just finished. It took me more than ten minutes just to make your plate. This is after I wake up early in the mornings and prepare for every day."

Saleem uncle picked up the plate and gazed around the stall.

"Son, you have to go out and hunt for a job. Look around my stall. Many other stalls sell pav bhaji now. I also have a lot of competition since I started the shop. I am struggling, but surviving."

"But who will give us a job?" Ratan asked in a frustrated tone.

"That I don't know. I only know how to run my snacks business. So many people come here, I listen to their talk while they sit here. I am just telling you what I have gathered from those chats. At the end of the day, it's upon the two of you and what you decide to do," saying this, Saleem uncle walked back at the counter to wash his hands.

Ratan looked at Ravi and asked curiously, "Do you know anyone who needs a permanent photographer? There is no harm in trying that out."

"Looks like you have taken uncle's words seriously. But yes, I agree, let's find some work. For now, I will park the idea of grocery stores." Ravi got up from the seat and washed his hands with a glass of water at the side of the table.

Ratan took out Rs. 100/- from the wallet, looked at uncle and said, "You are right, Saleem uncle, we need to find some work."

Saleem uncle took the money and said, "Yesterday a girl had come here. She was talking to someone about the requirement of a photographer. It was for a newspaper job. I just overheard her telling it to someone. If she comes tomorrow, I will give her your contact number in case she has some work for you," Saleem uncle smiled.

Ratan thanked uncle and walked toward the scooter. Ratan and Ravi never shied away from work. But how good they were at it, is something that they couldn't assess correctly. So even though they were hard-working people, they hardly got any work.

Ravi dropped Ratan and drove towards his home. His house was around a mile away from Ratan's. While he was taking a sharp turn near his place, another motorbike hit him head-on. The accident was not fatal, but still, it threw Ravi off the scooter a few feet away. He was lucky as his helmet had saved his head from hitting the wall, but he got a long scratch on his right forearm.

He stood up, limping, and straight away went to the man on the bike. Ravi held his neck and in anger, punched him on his head without realizing that the guy was wearing a helmet. The punch was so hard that it not only made his head quickly turn almost 90 degrees, but also made Ravi shout out in sharp pain.

The bike rider fell on the ground and tried to apologize. Ravi stopped and looked at him. Ravi guessed the guy must be in his late 50s. After taking a pause, Ravi shouted at that guy and swore viciously. The guy was quiet. He looked at Ravi with his helmet on and hands folded. Ravi calmed down and picked up his scooter. He warned him to ride the bike cautiously and drove his scooter home.

He reached home and looked at his fist. The fingers were swollen, with black-purple bruises on the skin. With his elbow, he pressed the doorbell. Ravi's mother opened the door and looked at Ravi's face which reflected his deep pain.

"What happened to you? Did you fall from the scooter? Didn't I tell you to ride the scooter cautiously? Where is Ratan? How is he? Is he fine?" Ravi was suddenly bombarded with questions.

"Mummy, you please take a break. I need some time to rest; don't ask me so many questions. Nothing happened," Ravi was holding his hand, and sat on the sofa.

"Look at your arm. It's bleeding. Tell me what happened. Let me bring a medical kit and also call Ratan," she went into the room to bring the medicine box and a glass of water.

"Don't call Ratan. He was not there when this happened. I took a turn in the last lane, and a motorcycle hit me from the front," Ravi groaned and picked up the glass of water and gulped it down.

"It must be your mistake. You don't ride the scooter properly. I always tell you to ride slow, but will you ever listen to me?"

"Okay, it's my mistake. Now no more argument, please," Ravi said submissively.

His mother knew that Ravi was in a temper, and he would never understand what was right at this point. She knew that if something made him angry, he would lose his cool and boil over quickly. So she called up Ratan and asked him to speak to Ravi the next day at the shop.

Ratan agreed. His mother had been standing behind him while he was talking on the phone.

"What happened?" she asked.

"Nothing! Ravi met with an accident after dropping me home. I will talk to him tomorrow," Ratan tapped his mother's shoulder lightly and walked towards the dining table.

"Nowadays you look worried, Ratan. If the shop is not generating enough revenue, why don't you try a new business?" his mother suggested.

"It will work mummy. And if not this business, then what other business can we do?" Ratan pulled the dining chair and sat down.

"There are many businesses you can do. For example, you could open a grocery shop," she said.

Ratan covered his face with both his hands and took a deep breath.

"Why is everyone in this world today giving me advice to open a grocery shop?" Ratan asked dejectedly, pulling the plate in front of him as he began to serve himself food.

His mother went inside the kitchen blabbering, "You never listen to my advice. Just like your father, he never used to listen to whatever I suggested."

Ratan looked at her walk inside the kitchen and started to eat his food.

The next day, in the shop, Ratan looked at Ravi's hand closely. "What happened?" he asked Ravi with suspicion.

"I hit someone on his head," Ravi replied.

"Why? Did you pick up a fight? But whoever he was, he must have been as fit as a butcher's dog. The punch has turned your fingers black and blue. Blood has clotted under the skin," Ratan said.

"He was wearing a helmet," Ravi said in disappointment.

"So?"

"I landed my punch on his helmet."

"What?" Ratan started to laugh like a maniac. "Why on the earth would you hit at something that was meant to protect you? That too, a helmet!"

After a few minutes, when Ratan had stopped laughing, he said, “See! When you lose your temper, your brain goes for a walk. Don’t worry; I will drop you off today. Don’t ride the scooter for a few days. Take rest.”

While they were talking about it, two men walked into the shop.

“Ratan baba! When will you pay the loan installment money? You have missed three installments to date.” The guy walked to the counter and peeked into the cash register to look for money while speaking to Ratan.

Ravi got up, but Ratan held him back and said, “We had an arrangement. There is still a week left. Will pay you before that.”

“Hmm, what happened to your hand Ravi?” he looked at Ravi and asked.

“I hit someone on his head,” Ravi swiftly responded with a dark look.

“No, no, he is just joking. He was testing how strong his helmet is,” Ratan said just before the man could react to Ravi’s statement.

The man chuckled and said, “Get some medicine for your hand as well as for your brain. Take my advice, treat your brain first, then your hand,” and walked out of the store.

“Three installments?” Ravi asked in disappointment and looked at Ratan.

“Yes, three installments. That is a total of Rs 1,25,000/-,” Ratan replied and went back to the cash counter. There were hardly a few hundred rupees.

Now they both started to think about the debt and how little time they had. G.B. studio was once again in trouble. This time, with the disappointed faces looking at each other, the shop looked gloomier.

That day no one came to the shop apart from the loan shark. Things were getting worse day by day, and they had no clue what to do next.

While going home, they stopped at Saleem uncle's shop.

"Look at yourself; I think you must close the shop for a few days. Take a break, go somewhere and come back again fresh," Saleem said.

"What? Till yesterday you asked us to find some work. Now you want us to take a break?" Ravi frowned.

"Son, you are like my kid. I can see how tense you are nowadays. I think if you take a break, you will get some time to think about yourself and the shop as well," Saleem said, gently tapping Ravi's shoulder.

"No uncle, we can't go anywhere. We have to pay three installments somehow, else we will be in deep trouble." Ratan said.

"Okay, as you both decide. Now show me your arms, quick." Saleem uncle asked both of them to fold their sleeves.

He pulled out two lockets looped in a black thread from his pocket and tied one on each of their arms.

"My nephew had recently visited Ajmer Sharif. I had asked him to bring this tabeez for both of you. It will help you in this time of crisis and will help you make better decisions. So don't take this off," Saleem tied the thread around their arms while chanting slowly. "Now let me go. You will soon find some work, Insha'Allah," saying this Saleem uncle walked towards the counter as another customer was there to pay the bill.

"One day, god will ask Saleem uncle why he wants to protect such useless fellows," Ravi chuckled and Ratan smiled.

On another side of the city, a guy of medium height, lean figure, in his early 50s, was limping with a slightly tilted neck towards a tea stall. He had many wrinkles on his face, which made him look much older than his age. His hair was all white and it was evident that he had had a much-troubled life. He was the same guy in the helmet whom Ravi had given a couple of knocks.

Limping, he walked towards the tea stall and asked the person sitting inside about the village Chanduali. The tea seller told him that Chanduali was around 120 km away from the city.

"That village is dreadful, sir. Why are you asking about it?" the tea seller asked surprised.

"What you have heard?" The guy asked him curiously.

"I have never been to that place, and I was born and raised here in this city. I have heard people say it is a hub of evil spirits. This is all because one tantric does some occult practices or some sort of black magic to speak to spirits. He has made them slaves. People say he can bring the dead to life too. If you are going into that village, please stay safe. There are rumors that people sacrifice humans as offering to him, sometimes to bring back the dead," he said in a worried voice as he handed over the teacup and continued, "Is there any problem with your neck, sir? Are you going there to fix your neck?"

The moment when he had been hit on his head flashed in front of him. With that, he got irritated.

"Mind your own business. I asked you where is Chanduali, and you told me. Now don't try to inquire more," he said in an angry voice.

"I was trying to help you, sir. But if you don't want to fix your neck, then why should I have any problem," the tea seller murmured and walked back to the tea stall.

The man got up and handed over a ten rupee note as he walked away. The tea seller looked at the middle-aged man, carrying a large backpack and trying his best to walk like a young and fit man, which he was not.

He took his bike and drove for around three hours to reach Chanduali. He never stopped on the way, even for a few minutes, and kept on going, nonstop. His neck and buttocks were hurting, but something pushed him to ride the bike nonstop to Chanduali without feeling any pain.

He reached the village and stopped his motorbike near a small shop. Without saying a word, he took out a piece of paper and showed the shopkeeper the name written on it. The shopkeeper looked terrified. He pointed towards a small hill, and while doing so, his whole body shook as if he had seen a ghost.

"You reach the foothill and ask someone. He stays in a cave there. You have to find his cave on your own. No one goes there," the shopkeeper said.

He thanked him, kept the paper back in his pocket, and drove his bike towards the hill. The road was full of pebbles, gravel, and broken stones. Driving the motorbike on that rickety road with the pain in the neck was hurting him. It was as if someone was pressing sharp needles into his neck.

After around an hour, he reached the bottom of the hill. It was so quiet that he could listen to the sound of his breathing. There was no one around. It was deathly silent with the sense of impending gloom. Now the challenging part was to find that cave. He parked his bike at the side of the hill and searched every nook and corner of the area. After looking around for an hour, he finally found a dark path that led to the cave, to the tantric.

The path was covered with bushes on both sides, with thorns and razor-sharp long grass. He used his jacket wrapped around his arms to move the bushes aside. Finally he reached the start of a tunnel. It was dark at the beginning of the tunnel, but he could see a fire burning inside it. He started to walk towards it. Inside the tunnel, the air was damp and cold, the smell around him was musty and moldy. Water streams covered part of the tunnel. Bats covered the cave's ceiling in patches, their poop scattered all over the floor. The air was warm with the smell of burning wood.

When he reached the fire, he saw a blind man; he looked like a tantric. As soon as he went closer, the tantric smiled.

"In your family, you are the second one to find me. First was your mother and now you. I know why you are here. Those ashes in your bag will not be of any help. The Kaal needs a living thing to help you. You need to find a heart—that heart which is made with her blood. Only then can I ask Kaal's help to bring her back. Go away! Remember when one human dies, another takes birth. You have to find her and take her heart out. Bring that heart here and take your love back," the voice echoed in the cave.

"I have searched for her everywhere, but all in vain, and I am tired now. Someone took her away a couple of months back. You need to help me here; Kaal needs to help me here. I came here with a lot of hope," he begged the tantric.

"You are asking a blind man to find something. Are you here to make fun of me?" the tantric yelled at him.

"No, no. I am here to seek help. You are a true worshipper of Kaal. He will listen to you. Please. Help me," the man replied.

The tantric put his hand in the fire and kept it there for a while. After a few minutes, he took out his hand and threw some powder-like substance in the air. He sniffed the air as if trying to decode something.

And then he said, "She is in the same city from where you just came. Surrounded by impenetrable walls, away from humans, breathing. Find her, Ajay. Kaal will always be with you,," saying this, the tantric became quiet.

"But where is she? Please tell me," Ajay begged again.

There was no reply. Ajay kept asking about her whereabouts, but the tantric didn't utter a word, as he went into deep meditation.

3
We Got a Job!

Two days later, in the G.B. studio, while Ratan was busy taking passport-sized pictures of a boy for exam hall entrance card, the phone rang. Saleem uncle was on the other side of the call. He told Ravi, "Yesterday evening, the girl came again. I have given your number to her. See if she has some job for you."

"Thanks, Saleem uncle, if she calls, we will speak to her," Ravi replied and hung up the phone.

That afternoon, Ratan received a call from her and she asked them to meet at Saleem uncle's stall around evening, as she had a job for them.

G.B. studio could finally see some light at the end of the tunnel. When they reached Saleem uncle's stall, they found uncle busy serving customers. After a few minutes, a soothing voice asked, "Are you guys Ratan and Ravi from G.B. photo studio?"

Ravi turned and saw a bubbly girl in a long black kurta and loose pajamas. Her brown hair cascaded down her shoulders. She had a saffron tint to her glossy skin.

Ratan looked at her and said, "Yes, we are Ratan and Ravi. Please have a seat."

Ratan looked at Ravi and coughed so that Ravi would take the hint and take his eyes off her.

"So, you guys run a photo studio. I came to know through Saleem uncle," the girl said.

"Yes, we do. We can do any jobs related to photo shoots," Ravi replied.

"I have an assignment to shoot the interiors of an old house," she offered.

Ravi was put off; he had thought that she wanted a photo shoot of herself. She added, "I am Aditi. I work for a local newspaper. Once you do the photo shoot, I'll write a story about it."

"Why do you need us? I'm sure you could take the pictures yourself. It seems simple enough," Ratan asked.

"I thought you guys needed work. If you are not interested, then let us end the conversation here," she replied with a deadpan expression.

"No, no, please. We need the job. We need one. Badly!" Ravi swiftly replied as she finished her statement.

Ratan leaned back in the chair and watched Ravi pacifying Aditi.

"There is no pressure. If you guys don't want to do it, I will find someone else," Aditi said, looking at Ratan.

"We will do it. We both will work on this project," Ravi said as Ratan watched and slightly moved his head.

That slight moment of the head was confusing. But the way Ravi was trying to convince Aditi, she understood it's a yes.

"Okay then. I will pick you up tomorrow from your studio, and we will go visit the house," Aditi said, holding the armrest of the chair and continued,

"I will go now. See you tomorrow."

"Join us for some pav bhaji," Ravi offered.

"No, thank you. I am good," Aditi replied and stood up to leave.

"How much will we be paid for this job?" Ratan asked in a low voice.

"You see the house first; then we can decide the amount," Aditi smiled and walked away.

"How can you talk to such a beautiful girl like this? She was giving us a job, and you are asking her to do it herself. How selfish you are!" Ravi said.

"Selfish? If I am asking her to do it by herself, how am I selfish," Ratan frowned.

"Didn't you notice my reaction when she walked up to us? And still, you wanted to let go of this opportunity?"Ravi said.

"Brother, looks are often deceptive," Ratan said.

"And how many such beautiful girls have you met in your life?" Ravi chuckled.

"Luckily, none!" Ratan smiled and said.

"Anyway, we need a job, and she has one." Ravi smiled and continued, "Now let's go, you have to drop me home."

While coming home, Ratan kept wondering why someone would need a photographer to shoot an old house.

They were still a week away from paying the installment to the loan shark. Would the money that Aditi pay be enough to buy more time? Since morning, he had been fiddling with the calculator. The new setup in the G.B. studio had cost them 5 lacs, and they had to pay it back in just a couple of months. The only blessing in disguise was that after this installment, only two were left, for which they could request an extension. Ratan's last hope was Saleem uncle if Aditi's assignment didn't work out. Ravi was busy spending time with the new digital camera they had bought.

"Look at the camera; it is up-to-snuff," Ravi said.

"It should be. We just bought it," Ratan replied.

"Yeah, true that. Do you want to shoot some pictures?" Ravi asked.

"No, it's fine. Anyway, today we have to see the house first."

"I don't expect much money from this job," Ravi said, looking at the camera.

Ratan nodded his head in agreement.

Around evening, Aditi walked into G.B. photo studio. She was dressed in a flowing kurta, long enough to cover her feet. Her hair was blowing in the air, and she looked stunning with that beautiful smile.

Ravi froze when he saw her. Ratan knew he would have to talk to Aditi as Ravi would take some time to regain his senses.

"You guys have a good shop. Everyone here knows about you," Aditi said, looking around the shop.

"Yes, it has been around for more than fifty years. Our fathers started it. They both were friends like us," Ratan replied.

"That's good. Shall we go now to see the house?" Aditi asked.

"Yeah, we are ready," Ratan looked at Ravi and coughed to catch his attention.

Ravi swiftly responded, "Yes, yes, let's go!"

"You don't have to take pictures today. Have a look at the house first, and then you can decide if you need more equipment to shoot," Aditi said.

"It is better to take some random pictures; this will give us an idea about what other things we need when we come next time," Ravi said.

While driving, Aditi said, "This story is crucial for me. I want you guys to capture the best possible pictures."

"Is the house occupied?" Ravi asked.

"It has been vacant for the last fifteen years."

"Where is it exactly?" Ratan asked.

"Have you seen the government veterinary hospital? It is close to its campus. I would say, just adjacent to it."

After driving for almost an hour through the traffic, they reached the periphery of the city. The campus was huge with vast lush green grounds and a small hospital building in one corner. Looking at the teenagers playing cricket in the ground, Ratan said,

"It's a fact that you don't realize that these are the best moments of your life."

They could see a small house across the field. Aditi drove her car through the road, and they reached a villa whose façade was almost hidden behind the tall Ashoka trees. It had a small gate through which the car could barely pass. Aditi slowed down the car and skillfully managed to get it in through the narrow gates. Looking at her expert navigation, Ratan asked, "Have you come here before?"

"No, never. I have passed by this road a couple of times but have never come inside," Aditi replied.

The house number hung loosely. "It's not 669. That number 9 is actually 6. The number is loose, and sometimes gets flipped. So it's 666/13B." Aditi smiled.

Ratan thought, *How come she entered so easily, unless she has driven here before? And how does she know that the number gets flipped, unless she has been here before? It's baffling!*

When the car stopped, Ravi came out of the car and looked around the house. The house had not been cleaned for ages. The paint was peeling off. Almost all the windows were closed and covered with cobwebs. Small plants popped out from the cracks and algae covered the facade. The villa was big. They had to walk a few meters to reach the door. Ratan was wondering what they would shoot inside the villa. He waited for Aditi to explain to them what exactly they needed to do. But in the first look itself, Ravi didn't have a good feeling about the house. He felt something was not right.

"It seems like no one has cleaned it up in ages. I am sure it would have been a stunning villa, but now it looks gloomy," Ratan said in a low voice, as if talking to himself.

"This house is still beautiful," Aditi looked at Ratan with a sober smile while walking towards the door.

Ratan didn't respond to that and kept walking, eyes glued to the gravel path. When they reached the door, Aditi saw a nameplate dangling on a nail, almost about to fall off. She pulled it off the wall and threw it in the dense bushes.

"What was that?" Ravi asked.

"It was loose and that could have fallen anytime. So, I threw it," she replied with a smile.

She reached the doorknob and tried to rotate it. But it was jammed. She looked at Ravi and said, "Do you want to try your luck?"

Ratan looked at Ravi's fingers, and shaking his head walked towards the door. He tried to push the knob. He was worried that if he put more pressure it would break.

He looked at Aditi and said, "I don't think this house has been empty since 15 years. It should be more than that. Look at the knob; it is completely rusted."

"We have to open it, Ratan. We have to go in," Aditi sounded anxious. Aditi's reaction firmed Ratan's belief that something was not right.

"Let me try again," Ratan said, and this time, he put as much pressure as he could, and the sound of a click was heard.

They thought that the door was open. Ratan smiled slightly and pushed open the door. But it was still locked.

They tried to move the knob again, but it was still locked.

"Did you also hear the sound of a click?" Ratan asked Ravi.

"Yes, I thought the door had opened." Ravi looked around. He saw a window open slowly. He tapped Ratan's shoulder and pointed to the window. Within seconds, the window closed with a bang. At that very moment, Aditi said in a loud and excited voice, "The door is open. I can rotate the knob."

Ratan was curious to know what precisely the job was, and it was now testing his patience. Finally, he said, "Before we go inside, you have to tell us what the job is all about. I am sure there is no electricity in the house."

"There must be, else we have the torch in our phones. And anyway, there's still sunlight."

"We will take some random pictures just to see how they turn out," Ratan replied.

"Yeah, you should. If your flash is on, then even in low light you can take some good shots," Aditi said.

Ravi told Ratan, "Let's go in and see."

Ratan was reluctant to go in, but he moved slowly towards the house. Light was coming through the cracks of the windows.

Once inside the house, Aditi asked, "Do you believe in ghosts or spirits?"

Ratan looked at Ravi, and Ravi replied, "Not until I see one."

Aditi gave a bizarre smile. Ratan and Ravi, without uttering a word, decided to ignore that reaction.

The wall was damp, and the musty smell in the room was powerful. They opened the window for ventilation.

"Aditi, what is the smell in the house? It's difficult to breathe. Absolutely no ventilation," Ratan said. Ravi took out the camera and started to scan the house through the lenses.

Aditi was moving around the house. Ravi could see the expression on her face, which told him how happy she was about the assignment and the place. Most of the time, he quietly focused his camera on her, not daring to click her pictures.

"See Ratan, it's her first assignment, and she wants to do her best. We should learn some dedication from this girl," Ravi tapped Ratan's shoulder and pointed towards Aditi.

"Yeah, but this is stinking a lot. Let's ask her what she needs to shoot, and then we can scoot from here," Ratan said, keeping one hand on his nose.

"Aditi, Aditi, please can you come here?" Ratan said in a loud voice.

"Yeah, what happened?" Aditi replied.

"What do we have to shoot? Let us know so that we can finish it and get out of this house. It's difficult to stand a minute here," Ratan said.

"Why? It's such a beautiful place," Aditi replied.

Ratan and Ravi looked at each other in surprise.

The design of the house was simplistic. The ground floor of the house had two rooms, a kitchen, and a big hall. There was a lot of furniture in the house, but it was half-covered with pieces of white cloth. Aditi climbed the stairs, and asked Ratan and Ravi to come up. They were reluctant, but followed her. On the first floor, there were two rooms and one big balcony. The stairs opened to the balcony. When Ratan reached the top, a gush of fresh air touched him on the face. Ratan took a deep breath and said, "Wow!"

"See, I told you. It is an amazing house," Aditi said.

One room on the left was completely pink. The walls, the bed, curtains, everything was pink. There were dolls arranged on the cupboard and a big teddy bear on the bed. It was so neatly arranged that no one could say that this house had been closed for so long. Aditi sat on the bed and looked up at the ceiling with a smile.

Ravi sat on another side of the bed near the teddy bear and said to Aditi, "You like this room!"

"Yes," Aditi replied in a low voice.

The sunlight was very faint, and the house was slowly becoming dark. Ratan came inside the room, looked around, and said, "Looks like someone arranged it just before we came."

"Yeah," Ravi replied and clicked some pictures of the room.

"I think we need to get going, it is getting dark," Ratan said.

"I will find the switchboard to turn on the lights," Aditi said and went down the stairs.

While Ratan and Ravi were in the room, an unfamiliar voice said, "You are hurting me, get up from the bed."

It sounded like a teenage girl in the room was speaking in a thin voice.

Ravi jumped off the bed, "Did you hear that?"

"Yes," Ratan paused and said.

"I swear if Aditi is joking with us. I will kill her!" Ratan said nervously.

Ravi said, "It must be Aditi joking. Look at my hand; it's sweating. Let's quickly move out of the house."

They heard Aditi's footsteps on the stairs.

Ravi and Ratan looked at each other. She was downstairs! Then whose voice was that?

Aditi walked into the room and said, "What happened to you guys? You look stunned. Look at yourselves."

After a minute, she said, "Let's go and see the other room. Then we can discuss what pictures we can take. Ravi has taken a few pictures, so he can suggest."

Ravi and Ratan quietly followed her. The room had a small bed with small toys scattered around. The color combination made it evident that it was intended for a baby boy.

Aditi went into the room, and quickly came out, "We are done. Let's go down and discuss more." It was evident that she didn't like the other room. They came down the stairs swiftly and stopped in the hall.

"How about this? You guys sit in the car. I will switch off the lights and join you in a while?" Aditi suggested.

While Ratan and Ravi were walking away, a voice seemed to whisper in their ear, "Bye bye!"

"Did you hear that?" Ravi asked.

"Yeah, but I felt it is the air making such sounds. Let's wait for Aditi in the car," Ratan said.

The lights of the house switched off and Aditi came out.

"Please tell me what's happening here?" Ratan asked Aditi.

Aditi looked at him and smiled, "Frankly, I didn't feel anything. But I know what you are asking. People around this place say that this house is haunted."

Ratan and Ravi shouted together, "What?"

Aditi smiled. "I don't believe in those stories. I have never felt anything like that. I have come here only once before, that too, not inside the house like today. Anyway, it's too late in the day, and I am hungry. Let's go to Saleem uncle's, and we can have the rest of the talk there."

She drove the car to Saleem uncle's place. Till they reached the shop, everyone in the car was quiet. Ratan was in this deep thought, thinking to himself.

"What is this job about? That gloomy house, mysterious voices. Why am I doing it? It's tough to keep the shop if I don't do this job, but I don't feel comfortable with this job. "

On the other hand, Ravi was baffled.

"So, it was a spirit that made that sound in the room, and not Aditi. And why would Aditi do that? After all, we are there to help her in her work."

After that long drive through the traffic, they reached Saleem uncle's shop. As usual, it was a bit crowded, but still, they managed to get a table for themselves.

As soon as they sat at the table, Ratan said promptly, "We will not do this job, Aditi. Period!"

Ravi and Aditi looked at Ratan. But Ravi knew what Ratan was thinking and it was hard for him to go against Ratan.

So, Ravi echoed his thoughts, "Aditi, that house is haunted. I told you that the window slammed, but you didn't hear it. Later someone in that bedroom asked me to move away from the bed. I thought it was you, kidding us, but no! Frankly, I don't believe in ghosts, but at the same time, "I am scared." Ravi said with a worried face. Only he knew how hard it was for him to say no to Aditi.

"Let's go, Ravi. We will find some way to settle the installment. Thanks Aditi," Ratan stood up and held Ravi's arm.

"How much do you guys have to pay?" Aditi asked with a poker face.

"It's none of your business Aditi. And that amount is huge. By any stretch of imagination, you won't give us that much for this simple but not so simple job. So, leave it!" Ratan replied.

"I understand. It's fine if you guys want to leave this job. But I am ready to pay you your fees. Whatever you guys have to pay as your installment," Aditi looked at Ravi.

"Can you pay us 1.25 lacs," Ratan asked rather hotly, expecting Aditi to back off from her words.

"Yes, I will," Aditi replied with a smile.

Stunned, Ratan looked at Ravi. "Ravi, I told you from the start, I don't have a positive feeling about this job. Now see, there is a ghost. Is this the only adventure left in our lives? I am not doing this. Let's go," Ratan tapped Ravi's shoulder.

Ravi looked at Aditi and said, "I can't leave Ratan. Sorry Aditi, we can't take this job."

"I like your bromance. But how about a story over pav bhaji. Listen to it, and if you still don't want the job, then we split our ways," Aditi said.

Ravi said, "What do you say Ratan?"

Ratan looked at Ravi and shook his head. "Fine! I am all ears."

Aditi looked towards Saleem uncle and waved her hand to order three plates of pav bhaji. Then she looked at both of them, Ravi and Ratan. "Thank you for listening to me. This is a story about a couple who loved each other a lot but could not be with each other. This is the story of the villa which became haunted after two mysterious deaths," Aditi began.

4
Operation 'Heart'

Ajay Rajput had just passed out of medical college. He had come to this city in the 1980s. He longed to be a famous consultant surgeon one day.

A consultant surgeon is the most senior surgeon in the hospital. He aimed to specialize in heart surgery, so he joined the city's prominent Gangaram Hospital as a core training doctor. The hospital was currently going through a financial crisis. It was heavily dependent on the trustees and other investors. The recent fraud in the hospital had caused a heavy dent in the hospital's image, which made two of the investors pull out from the Board.

Dr. Ajay was around 31 years old when he came to the hospital. He was assigned to assist Dr. Manju Mehta, who was five years older than him. Ajay had spent most of his early life in the village. His father was a farmer and worked on contract farming for other zamindars. They were exploited and left with very little savings. Whatever little they had saved, was spent on Ajay's education. A considerable loan was also taken, which Ajay paid back by working at the hospital. To ensure that Ajay received a good education and did well, Ajay's mother visited sadhus and aghoris. She was doing all she could to take Ajay out from that bog of poverty. In reality, Ajay didn't need anything of that sort; he was born talented and was ready to take on the world.

Ajay was hardworking and kept honesty as a top priority in his life. Even if he spoke to someone senior, he didn't hesitate to tell the truth, no matter how bitter it was. His colleagues often repeated Ajay's favourite line, "If you do easy work, your life becomes hard. And if you work hard, your life becomes easy."

After few years of working as an assistant in the hospital, he got promoted to an associate specialist surgeon in his department. From working as an assistant to Dr. Manju Mehta, he was now her peer.

Everything was going well until the day they received a high-profile surgery case. The hospital board directed the consultant surgeon to assemble the best team. After all, they were performing surgery on one of the trustees, Mr Ramchandani. The surgery was expected to last more than 12 hours. Ajay was also picked up to be part of the core team performing the surgery. Everything in the hospital was to be inspected thoroughly, right from oxygen cylinders to electricity backup. Even the pieces of cotton were counted and supplied in excess to ensure nothing would go wrong. The hospital blood bank had been informed. If this surgery was successful, it would make headlines. It was not only a chance for doctors to do their best, but also to become superstars overnight. The date of surgery was after a week.

After a few days, Dr. Manju Mehta called Ajay in her cabin.

She said to Ajay, "There is a lot to learn from you, Ajay. And you also have a lot to learn too. I mean as a surgeon. But as a human being, you have reached the pinnacle already. I am very impressed with the way you handle patients in the hospital. Now, I want to share some news with you. You know the case of Mr. Ramchandani, who is going in for a Septal Myectomy to unclog the muscles of the heart."

Dr. Ajay replied, "Yes, and the heart will be motionless when we operate."

"True, for five to six hours, he will be in the ICU with his heart beating a few feet away. Outside of the body. You, Ajay, are the only person who can manage the blood flow in crucial heart surgeries with the heart-lung machine," Dr. Manju Mehta smiled and continued, "You have been chosen to be a part of the surgical team."

Dr. Ajay smiled and replied, "Thanks, Dr. Manju. I know you must have proposed my name. "

"That doesn't matter. You are doing a great job in the hospital. So we all recognize your efforts. This is the reason you are on the team. All I have done is remind them and the decision was unanimous," Dr. Manju walked to Dr. Ajay, held his hand and continued, "Give your best Ajay; it is a golden chance for you and everyone at Gangaram."

Dr. Ajay felt the warmth of her hands. He was quiet and nodded his head. He blushed. Dr. Manju noticed the way Ajay's body reacted to her touch. She slowly turned and sat on her chair.

"I know you will do your best, Ajay," she said.

Ajay thanked her and went back to his cabin.

The surgery was planned for Sunday. It was now three days away. Dr. Ajay knew that he would not be alone in the room on the day of the surgery, but what if he could not do his part. He turned quieter than usual, repeatedly bit his nails, and moved in the corridors with deep thoughts. Dr. Manju noticed this change and felt that it was not a good sign.

That evening, a day before the surgery, she called Dr. Ajay to her cabin. Dr. Ajay was quiet. Dr. Manju sat near him and said, "Ajay, listen. I can see you are worried. This is neither good for you, nor for the team. Especially now when something big is going to happen in your life."

"I don't know if I will be able to do it. I am feeling nervous. Look at my hands," he said as he held his shaking hands in the air.

Dr. Manju smiled and said, "Once you overcome your fear, you will experience the best moment of your life, the accomplishment of a job well done. Believe in god and yourself and see all the wonderful things that will happen to you."

Dr. Manju held Ajay's hand and said, "Be confident in what you do and don't worry. Things will be all right."

Dr. Ajay felt much better. He could feel all his worries vanish instantly, and what remained with him was the beautiful moment and that mushy feeling.

The day finally arrived. Every staff was present in the hospital. It was around a 12-hour marathon. Dr. Ajay saw a CD player in the OT, which was baffling. Later he got to know that Dr. Mitra, consultant surgeon, played instrumental music during the surgery. Dr. Ajay had heard that consultant surgeons usually listened to music while in the surgery, but he had never seen it before.

Dr. Manju came to Dr. Ajay and said, "Make sure you keep that smile on your face and your mood light. In the OT, stress is not allowed. If Dr. Mitra even gets a hint that you are under stress, he will not allow you to be there. Remember what I said. Overcome your fear."

After an hour, around 10 am, Mr. Ramchandani was brought into the OT. He was young, good-looking, with an angular face. Ramchandani was awake as he was wheeled in. He did not smile, but didn't look worried either. He was one of the top businessmen in the city. After all the staff had entered the OT, the room was locked. The anesthetist came forward to help Mr. Ramchandani go into a deep sleep. In a matter of minutes, he was lying on the surgery bed like a log. Dr. Mitra switched on the CD player, and instrumental music started playing. He was famous for keeping the mood light inside the OT.

Reporters from magazines and newspapers had started to reach the hospital. Around noon, Dr. Mitra called Dr. Ajay. He was standing behind the anesthesia machine. Dr. Manju could see Dr. Ajay walking in with confidence. Dr. Ajay looked at Dr. Manju and went near the heart-lung machine. The system was switched on, and blood started to flow through it. Now, the heart was made motionless and ready to operate. Time passed, and no one came out of the OT. Around 2 pm, the electricity went off and there was panic everywhere. The news spread like wildfire. But in the OT, things were normal as all the equipment was connected to the generator, even Dr. Mitra's CD player. The staff in the OT were unaware of the chaos amongst reporters outside the hospital. The only thing which stopped was the airflow. It could be dangerous as infection in the room could quickly spread in the OT. The hospital lobby started to move quickly to bring up electricity. After a few minutes, the electricity was back and everyone was relieved. When the muscle was taken out of the heart's deepest layer, Dr. Mitra asked Dr. Ajay to bring back the blood flow to the heart. Dr. Ajay slowly operated the machine. The heart was pumping and live again. Dr. Mitra smiled at Dr. Ajay and went back near the patient.

Around 7 pm, as soon as Dr. Mitra came out of the OT, all the reporters surrounded him. He took off the surgical cap, mask and said, "It is successful, and Mr. Ramchandani is doing well."

There were claps of joy and smiles all around. It was not only Dr. Mitra or his team's success, but the entire hospital had waited with bated breath to know the result of the surgery.Newspapers, the next day, were covered with the surgeons' pictures.

Mr. Ramchandani was kept in the ICU and closely monitored by Dr. Manju.

Within a few days, Mr. Ramchandani had recovered a lot. Dr. Manju was closely monitoring his health. It didn't take long for Mr. Ramchandani to realize how important Manju had become for him.

On his rounds to check up on Mr. Ramchandani, Dr. Ajay noticed the way he interacted with Dr. Manju. He felt it was important for him to tell Manju about his feeling towards her.

That day Dr. Ajay and Dr. Manju came out of Mr. Ramchandani's room together.

"Dr. Manju, it has been a tiring day. How about a cup of coffee? I also have to talk to you about something. Personal!" Ajay asked Manju while walking down the alley.

Manju had an inkling that Ajay might express what he felt about her.

"Yeah, sure. Hospital canteen?" Manju asked.

"How about a drive a few minutes away from here? There is one Gully's Café," Ajay asked with a smile on his face.

Manju was impressed by Ajay's confidence and said, "Why not?"

They came out of the hospital holding their white lab coats in their hands.

Manju took the car, and Ajay sat beside her. Finally, they reached Gully's Café. Ajay swiftly went inside the café to grab the corner most seat. "Dr. Manju, I want to talk to you about something very personal. So, I decided to bring you here."

"Yes, that's fine. Now, tell me what you want to say."

"Dr. Manju, thanks for all that you did for me. I mean, proposing my name for the team and your confidence in me. I mean, I couldn't have done it without your support. I mean..."

Dr. Manju cut him off and said, "Just say it. What do you actually mean?"

Suddenly a waiter came to their table.

"Can I take your order, sir?" he asked.

"No, not at the moment, please," Ajay said and waited for the waiter to go away.

"Ajay! You have to be quick,"Manju said.

Ajay cut her off in between and said, "Love you!"

She looked at Dr. Ajay and said, "Sorry I didn't hear you properly. What did you just say?"

"Manju, let me try it again. It was all normal when I joined Gangaram. But something happened when I met you. Slowly I found that spending time with you was the only thing I wanted. Sometimes I wanted to meet you, and you were busy. I felt embarrassed that I wanted your attention. It didn't take me much time to realize that I want to spend the rest of my life with you. That's it, I guess. Now, before that waiter comes back again, I want to say... I love you!" Ajay looked at Manju and waited for her reaction.

"I knew it was coming, Ajay. I need some time to think,"Manju looked at her watch.

Ajay anxiously asked in a low voice, "How much time?"

"Ten seconds!" she paused for a few seconds and looked into Ajay's eyes.

She broke into a laugh and said,

"I was waiting for that idiot!" Ajay blushed and got up from his seat. He went down on his knees, held her hand and said, "I will love you with everything I have. Every single day! No matter what."

Ajay looking into her wet eyes and kissed her hand.

Back at the hospital, Mr. Ramchandani had recovered quite a bit. Doctors suggested that he be discharged, and Mr. Ramchandani also wanted to get back to his business. But there was one last thing that remained. On his last day in the hospital, Manju's room was filled with a bouquet of red roses. She was amazed to see the room covered in red. Thinking that Ajay had sent the flowers, she smiled to herself.

With that thought, she reached her desk where she saw a beautiful greeting card.

The note read, "Thanks for all the love and care you have given me! I am indebted to you."

Manju smiled as she looked at the bottom right corner of the note, "My life is yours, Manju. Ram (Ramchandani)!"

Her smiling faded, and she asked herself in a low voice, "Ramchandani? Why?"

She walked towards Ramchandani's room.

He was reading a magazine. As soon as he saw Manju walking towards him, a beautiful smiled broke on his face.

He asked, "Did you like the flowers?"

With a strained smile, Manju said, "Yeah, they are very beautiful."

"Not more than you," Ramchandani said as he sat up on the bed and continued further.

"I know what you are thinking, Manju. See, I am very shy with women; unless it's business. When it comes to expressing what's in my heart, I simply can't. I just don't have the courage. A pure businessman only knows how to treasure money, not the heart. But things changed when you were around. I have fallen for you, and I can't help it. I had never thought that I would find love in a hospital. I believe the money I invested in this hospital has given me such a beautiful gift. Tell me Manju, would you like to spend your life with me?"

Manju didn't expect this. She was shocked to know the depth of Ram's feelings towards her. She was worried that if she refused his proposal, he could potentially stop the funding. After all, he was one of the trustees of the hospital. Suddenly, the faces of all staff members flashed in front of Manju.

"What are you thinking, Manju? I am very sorry if you didn't like what I said. But I can't help it. It is what it is. This heart needs care by the one who helped it beat again. I hope you will make sure it doesn't break," Ramchandani smiled.

Manju said, "Yes, I must keep it healthy. It is a big decision for me to take. I will think about your proposal Ram sir."

As she turned to go out of the room, Ram said, "I hope that you will say yes, Manju. For me," he took a pause, and Manju turned back and looked at him. He continued, "And for the hospital," he smiled.

Manju nodded her head and walked out of the room.

She went to her cabin, and the phone rang.

"Hello Manju, someone told me you had your cabin full of roses. Who is this lover boy?" Ajay chuckled and continued, "Okay, leave it. Let's go for dinner tonight?"

"I will call you back, Ajay. Need to go for my rounds," Manju said and kept the receiver down.

She faced a fork in the road. The first one led to a beautiful life she had always dreamt of. The other was like a blackboard in a dark room. She would have to build the relationship by shattering two hearts. Most importantly, it was the staff who would suffer in this story. While she was in this deep thought, a nurse walked in. "Madam, may I speak to you for a minute. Please."

"Yes, Sarla, please come in. Sit!" Manju pointed at the chair.

"Madam, I need some help. I have heard that my salary this month will be withheld because I hadn't submitted the reason for the urgent leave I had taken. Please, can you ask the admin department to release the payment? I have to buy some medicines for my husband. You know how critical it is. Please, can you help me?" she begged Manju.

"Yes, I will. Don't worry. I will speak to them," Manju stood up and ushered Sarla outside the cabin.

Due to the cash crunch, Gangaram Hospital was being harsh on the staff. Scrutiny was at its peak; any inconsistency was straightaway impacted by salary cuts. So either it was delayed, or the staff received a pay cut. Sarla was one of the victims.

This small incident turned Manju's mind into accepting Ramchandani's proposal.

She got up and went to Dr. Mitra's cabin. "Dr. Mitra. Remember you spoke about the camp in the Bastar area. I have spoken to Dr. Ajay. He will go there."

"You do know that this assignment is at least for three months?" Dr. Mitra asked.

"Yes, I know."

"I will let the camp know about Dr. Ajay."

"Thanks, Dr. Mitra," Manju said.

She dialled Ajay's cabin. "Ajay, do you remember about that camp in Bastar that Dr. Mitra was talking about? Can you go there? Please, for me?" she begged in a shallow voice.

"No. I don't want to be away from you. I can't," Ajay replied.

"It's important, Ajay. You know what's happening there," Manju paused for few seconds and replied, "Sometimes people need us in their lives. And we should support them, whether as doctors or as humans. God often gives us a key to their wellbeing and happiness. We should do what it takes; it's a big responsibility."

"But, Majnu...."

Manju cut Ajay in between, "Don't say no Ajay. Please. I will join you there in a few days."

"I won't argue then. Okay, my princess. As you say. But promise me, you'll be there soon."

Manju crossed her index and middle fingers together and said,

"Yes, I will be there."

With that empty promise, she closed her eyes, and tears rolled down her cheeks onto the crossed fingers. She murmured slowly, "I am sorry, Ajay, I am sorry."

Ajay left for Bastar after a couple of days. Manju accepted Ram's proposal, and they got married. After the marriage, Ram told the Board of Directors to pay three times the bonus to all the staff. After a few days of marriage, Manju came to the hospital to meet the team. Each and every staff member came to greet Manju. The hospital, which had been on the verge of sinking, now had the confirmed support of Ram, thanks to Manju.

While she was in her cabin, Sarla came in, "Madam, may I come in?"

"Yes, Sarla. Please come in."

"Many congratulations, madam. And thank you."

"Thank you? For what?"

"You know, due to Ramchandani sir's big heart, I was able to pay all my loans. Ramchandani is god for us. It's all because of you. Thank you, Madam."

Dr. Manju smiled wanly. She alone knew what all she had given up to give people like Sarla the life that they wanted. It was an unsaid sacrifice, of which the staff would never know.

Ajay had come to know about Manju's marriage to Ramchandani. He was shattered to the core and was not able to accept why Manju had done that. Ajay decided that he would not go back to the city again and would remain at Bastar for his entire life. He never called up Manju to know the reason behind her decision. Neither did Manju reach out to Ajay to explain why she took that decision.

Years passed. Manju struggled to keep her married life on track. Ram's business had gone south, and his health too. Mounting pressure from the bank and new emerging technologies gave him a tough time. More and more Chinese firms were flooding the retail shops with cheap products. Things went from bad to worse, and he had to sell off all his properties to pay the debt. Manju, being an established doctor, was the primary breadwinner of the house. God had blessed them with one princess just after marriage. Ram had wanted a boy. He believed that a male child could take his business ahead. He was so obsessed with having a boy that he had decorated one of the rooms all in blue, even before they could conceive.

He hated their daughter Hema. His behavior was psychologically impacting Hema; she was having trouble sleeping. The only way Manju let Hema sleep was by telling her stories or sometimes giving her a medicine to make her sleep. At that age, it was a crime to give her sleeping pills. It was the worst thing Manju had faced in her life. So the looming question was, how to protect Hema?

One day, Ajay came to the city. An NGO had invited him to facilitate him for his work towards the tribes of Chhattisgarh. Ajay was in the local news, and everyone knew about his arrival into the city, including Manju and Ram.

Dr. Mitra requested Ajay, via the NGO, to meet him in the hospital. Ajay agreed after a lot of reluctance. Ajay had changed a lot; he had a long beard, wore a kurta, and carried a bag that had some books related to tribal and herbal medicine.

"Dr. Ajay, you have done a fantastic job at Bastar. I will not be surprised if you stand for the election and win it. And look at you! You have changed so much," Dr. Mitra chuckled.

"Thanks, Dr. Mitra. I have learned immensely from you. And everything that I learned here helped me at Bastar. I have started to live a simple life Dr. Mitra; it helps me in connecting with the local people there," Dr. Ajay replied.

"Good. Let me ask Dr. Manju to join us. Have you guys met? She was the one who told me that you were interested in going to Bastar. You must be in touch, right?" Dr. Mitra picked up the phone and called Dr. Manju.

Ajay gave a surprised look. Why did Manju send me to Bastar? Is it so that she could marry Ramchandani?

"What happened, Ajay?" Dr. Mitra looked at Ajay's expression.

"Nothing, doctor. Nothing at all," Dr. Ajay smiled.

Dr. Manju walked into the room. Ajay was a completely changed man from what he used to be. Her heart started to beat faster, and she almost fumbled, "H..ha...hi Ajay."

Ajay looked at her and smiled. Then, he said, "Hello, Dr. Manju. It has been long."

Dr. Manju sat on the chair just beside him and said, "Yes, it has."

"Dr. Ajay has changed the lives of the people of Bastar.

This country needs people like you. I hope others get inspired by you," Dr. Mitra said.

"Thanks to Dr. Manju. If you had not been there, I wouldn't have been able to do so much," he said, looking at Manju.

The phone rang, and Dr. Mitra answered it.

"Yes, I will be there!" He kept the receiver down, looked at Ajay, and walking out of the room said, "Stay here, Ajay. I will be back in a moment." Ajay and Manju were alone in the room. Even though they were sitting in close proximity, the gap between them was so deep that it would take a lifetime to fill it.

"How are you?" Manju asked.

"I don't know. It has been long since I have asked myself this," Ajay chuckled.

"You have changed a lot," Manju said in a fumbling voice.

"I am the same. The world around me has transformed a lot. The way people perceive me has changed."

"You were never so philosophical," Manju chuckled as she wiped away her tears.

"How are you, Manju? I hope Ram is keeping you happy."

"I am sorry Ajay, I am so sorry," Manju started crying, covering her face with both hands.

Ajay got up from his seat and got down on his knees, "Don't say sorry, Manju. I believe our love was strong and pure. I trusted you then; I trust you now. I don't want to know what happened. I always kept you in my prayers."

He took a handkerchief and wiped away her tears.

"Did you get married?" Manju asked.

"No, I have loved only you."

"I want to talk to you, Ajay. Can we meet again?" Manju asked.

"Do you want to meet? Will that make you happy?" Ajay asked in a low voice.

Manju nodded her head.

"Then let's meet at Gully's. I have heard that it's a big restaurant now," Ajay said.

Manju nodded her head, wiping away her tears.

Ajay sat back on the chair, and Dr. Mitra walked in. "Sorry, guys," and smiled.

They all talked for some time, and Ajay left the hospital to return to his hotel room. After this meeting, he told himself that no matter what Manju said to him, he would not come back to this city. Manju has chosen a life for herself and Ram and she were happy. His presence in the town may cause turbulence in her life, which Ajay would never like.

The next day at Gully's, Manju came early and waited for Ajay. She was anxious, but trying hard to hide it from the people around her. She kept on looking at the door. After a few minutes, Ajay walked in quietly and tapped Manju's shoulder.

"Ram is lucky. A lady who fixed his heart and now his life. What else could anyone want?" Ajay said.

"Things were not the same after you went to Bastar. Or should say, when I sent you there," Manju said in a shaky voice, and Ajay looked at her soulful eyes.

Manju told Ajay how things had changed. Ram was almost broke, and his obsession for a male child was driving her crazy. The only reason Manju didn't want to leave Ram was because of his poor health. Ajay was disappointed to see that what he had thought to be a perfect marriage was actually a dreadful compromise.

"What is her name Manju?"Ajay asked her about her daughter.

"We call her Hema. She is the only good thing that has happened to me," Manju smiled.

"Nice name; it must be your choice," Ajay said, to which Manju nodded.

"Ajay, I need one help," Manju asked with both her hands wrapped around Ajay's hand.

"Yes, tell me," Ajay replied.

"Can you take Hema with you? I am worried if she stays here, Ram's attitude will hurt her psychologically and impact her growth," Manju said.

"Okay, but I can't simply take her away from you both. Will Hema want to come with me? And where will I take her. I am in Bastar. There is nothing much there. In the city, she can have a better education and life," Ajay replied.

"No, Ajay, please promise me that you will take her with you. Her mental growth is getting significantly impacted; her life will become hell," Manju started to weep again.

"But Manju..."

Manju stopped Ajay, "Don't say no, Ajay. Please! I know you have done a lot for me. Please, can you do it for my daughter?"

Ajay had never imagined seeing Manju in such a sad state. Even though their paths were separate, but Manju was still in his heart.

Ajay took a deep breath and said, "I will take Hema with me."

Ajay had never thought his life would take such a turn when he returned to the city.

The next day, Ajay was at the NGO conference where he was awarded. After the award ceremony, Manju picked up Ajay from the event and took him home. But, when they reached, Ram was not happy to see Ajay there. After greeting

Ajay, he stepped out with the pretext of some work. He was so aggravated that he forgot that Ajay was the same doctor who had kept his heart beating in that crucial surgery.

Manju found it an excellent opportunity to introduce the eight-year-old Hema to Ajay. "What a beautiful princess! Hello Hema!" Ajay said to Hema.

Hema smiled and said, "But Papa says that I am not a good girl because I am not letting his prince come home. Not sure why Papa says like that! Papa doesn't love me."

Ajay went close to Hema, kept his hand on her head, and said, "Let's go and find your Papa's prince. Will you come with me? This will make your Papa happy."

It was hard for Manju to let Hema go with Ajay. But other than this, what option did she have? Manju quickly packed Hema's bag. Ajay looked at Hema and said, "Don't worry, Hema, Mummy will be with us soon."

As Manju heard those words, her conversation with Ajay where she had convinced him to go to Bastar flashed before her eyes. Manju took Hema's bag and went to the car. Ajay holding Hema's hand, walked out of the house. It was hard for Manju even to look at Hema leaving. They all sat in the car and left for the airport.

A couple of days later, after Hema had left with Ajay, he got the shocking news that Manju and Ram were found dead in their house. The cause of death was unknown. After that incident, people said that the house was abandoned as no one wanted to stay there. Thus, the beautiful story of Ajay and Manju had ended tragically. Ajay couldn't believe that Manju would leave him so soon.

5
Invisible Host

Aditi had completed her story. She was quiet and stared at the table with both hands folded. It was almost midnight. All the clients at Saleem uncle's were gone. He had also joined them to listen to Ajay and Manju's story.

To break the silence, Ratan said, "So, you need the pictures of the house to publish Manju and Ram's story."

"Manju lost everything. Ajay, Hema.... I want to write about her, about her sacrifice. But no one wants to come with me in the house because of the ghost," Aditi said.

"Whose ghost?" Ratan asked.

"Manju or Ram, probably," Aditi replied.

"Then why are they scaring people away?"Ratan asked.

"I am telling *their* story, Ratan. Why will they scare you off?" Aditi asked.

"What about the banging of the window flap, the voice in the bedroom and someone whispering bye-bye to us?" Ravi asked.

"What rubbish! I haven't heard anything like that. But maybe they want you to know about their presence," Aditi replied.

"Aditi, wait a minute. I am not able to understand this. Manju and Ram are dead. They had issues in their marriage. Fine. I mean, not fine. Anyway, leave that! Later they died.

Story ends. What do they want to tell us? Their marriage was hell anyway, and it had a terrible ending, "Ratan said.

"See, guys, I don't believe there is any ghost. And if there is, they may want to talk about how they died. So that's it," Aditi said.

"So, you want us to shoot some pictures of that house?" Ratan asked.

"For me, paying that installment is scarier than going into that house," Ravi replied.

Aditi looked at both of them.

"So, now you know the entire story. We must discuss the fee for this job. So, it's a deal, then?"

Ravi smiled, "Yes," and looked at Ratan.

Ratan took a deep breath and said, "I don't have an option."

Aditi stood up and said, "Good then, let me solve your problem first; then you can solve mine. I will come back to you tomorrow with the cheque for the full amount. Day after tomorrow, we go back to the house."

Ravi smiled when he heard that they would get the cheque tomorrow. But the expression on Ratan's face told a different story. He was still not convinced why Aditi was paying such a massive amount, only for taking the pictures for her story. She could easily handle that herself. He was sure there was more going on here than met the eye. Ravi tapped Ratan's shoulder and said, "Let's go; it is very late"

When Ravi and Ratan started to walk towards their scooter, Saleem uncle asked, "Ravi, Ratan, do you have that thread around your arms?"

Both of them touched their arms and said, "Yeah, we do. Why?"

"Nothing! Don't worry about that ghost," Saleem uncle smiled.

Ravi shrugged. Ratan smiled, kept both his hands on Saleem uncle's shoulder, and said, "Thanks Saleem uncle. If you are there, nothing will happen to us."

Saleem smiled and said, "Goodnight! May god bless both of you."

"Goodnight uncle," Ratan said, and both of them came back home.

Ratan couldn't sleep that night. He was a firm nonbeliever of supernatural powers. He decided that he would go alone to the place the next day.

The next morning, Ratan texted Ravi that he would come late to the shop. Ratan reached the haunted house. He parked the bike on the campus and looked at the building. It was the same gloomy feeling he had the first time. The leaves of the Ashoka trees rustled due to the heavy winds. While he was slowly walking towards the main door, he could hear his shoes crushing against the gravel on the pathway.

He expected the doorknob to be jammed. To his surprise, it opened without any effort. That surprised Ratan; he frowned and looked at the knob. Through squinted eyes, he looked at the open window flap, half expecting it to slam. It didn't move an inch, despite the wind.

He quietly stepped inside the house, into the main hall. He looked around and shouted, "Is anyone there?"

There was a faint echo as the place was empty.

Suddenly, he noticed pictures of a couple on the table. It looked like Manju and Ram. He could see the same couch, now covered with white cloth behind him. Ratan picked up the picture, wiped it with his palm, and kept it in his shirt pocket.

He heard a door of the room on the first floor. His heartbeat spiked, and he started to breathe heavily. He looked at the curved stairs going up. Ratan decided to go up. Finally, he got to the passageway to the top floor. The door of the pink room on the left was open. He looked at the closed door on the right.

In a shaky voice, he asked, "Anyone there?"

Ratan tried to open the door, but it was locked. He felt as though someone had locked the room from inside. He knocked on the door. He could feel someone inside moving very slowly.

He walked into the pink room. Looking around, he sat on the bed near the teddy bear. Suddenly a voice said, "You are hurting me; get up from the bed." It was the same voice that he had heard earlier when he was with Ravi in the room.

He decided to rush out of the house. As soon as he opened the door, a faint voice said, "Bye-bye!" It was the same voice that they had heard the last time they were there. He ran towards the bike. As he turned around for one last look, his hair stood on end. He could see a shadow at the window. Rushing out, he saw a man sitting near the gate. He was all black – the cloth, the skin color, with messy hair and beard. At a glance, he seemed like a beggar. He looked at Ratan and laughed maniacally.

Back in the shop, Ravi was eagerly waiting for Aditi. The second reason was the cheque he was about to receive, but the first and primary reason was that he would be with Aditi alone in the shop.

Around noon, he saw Aditi walking in. As soon as she opened the door, the room filled with the fragrance of her perfume. Ravi looked at Aditi and took a deep breath. Aditi reached Ravi and asked, "Where is Ratan?"

"Ratan is not around. He will be late today. You look stunning as usual. How has your day been so far?" Ravi smiled.

"Nothing much. I took a break today. It has been tiring since the last couple of days, so I thought of taking a day off," Aditi replied with a smile.

"Anyway, I have brought the cheque Ravi. Tell me, against whose name do you want it? "

"You can write anyone's name. Mine or Ratan's. Which one do you want?" Ravi asked slowly.

"Anyone," Aditi replied.

Ravi asked again, "Anyone?" expecting Aditi to choose his name.

"Yeah, anyone," Aditi paused and said, "Okay, tell me your full name."

Ravi blushed and replied, "Yes, sure! It is Ravi Bhagat."

Aditi wrote Ravi's name on it and said, "I have written the cheque in your name. Now, do you want me to drop it for you?" Aditi smiled.

"I can deposit it in the branch. It's okay," Ravi said.

Aditi hesitated. She looked at Ravi with a sudden change in expression, and with the sweetest smile asked him, "Did you have your lunch?"

Ravi was puzzled by the change. He stammered, "No, not yet."

"Then let's get some lunch and then we can go together to the bank and drop the cheque. What say?" Aditi asked Ravi.

His heart danced with joy as he replied, "Yes, yes, it would be my pleasure, Aditi."

Ravi took out the keys to close the shop. Then he realized that Ratan may come anytime. He was in a dilemma, and decided to text Ratan, "Hey, going out for lunch. Closing shop for a while and will be back soon. See you!"

Aditi was in the car, waiting for Ravi.

She asked, "So, any place you want to pick?"

"Aditi, I want to share something with you. I have never been with a girl before. I mean, I don't have any experience of which place they would like. So please, you choose the place."

Aditi laughed, "Don't be shy Ravi. I am okay with any place you select."

Ravi thought to himself, *"Ravi, what will you do now? You have never been to any place other than Saleem uncle's. Pray to God and pick any one of the nice restaurants on the way. Impress her."*

"So, anything you can think of?" Aditi asked.

Ravi looked at Aditi. She was a completely different person from when he had met her last. She was blushing, smiling, talking. Ravi felt that he was talking to a different person and not Aditi. Whoever she was, Ravi was enjoying her priceless company.

"I have one place I can think of. I am sure you will like it," Ravi smiled and said.

After a drive of twenty minutes, they reached a restaurant that had a tiny counter and kitchen inside the building. All the chairs and tables were outside on the small lawn. A plastic rope was tied to the restaurant's board and hung with a nail to prevent it from falling.

The name of the restaurant was Lash (dead body).

Aditi looked at it and said, "Is this the restaurant?"

"Yeah, this is the one. But, the name board is broken. The name is actually Kailash," Ravi replied with a smile.

They both sat down.

"What would you like to have, Aditi?" Ravi asked.

"I would go with a diet coke and vegetarian thali," Aditi replied.

"Sounds good! I will go with the same," Ravi chuckled.

They both laughed.

While eating, Ravi asked, "Since how long have you been in this city? Since childhood?"

"No, I came here a few years back."

"With your parents?"

"No, I am alone. I lost both of them in an accident very early in my life. An orphan in this city!"

"Oh, I am sorry to hear that," Ravi said.

"Don't be sorry," Aditi smiled and went quiet for a while and then continued.

"The world teaches you the best lessons of your life when you are alone."

Ravi quietly listened. He saw a lonely person in Aditi, someone completely different from the girl he was beginning to know. It might be the trauma of losing her parents early in life.

After a few minutes, Ravi said, "I hope we could help you with your assignment."

"Which assignment?" Aditi asked.

"The photography job," Ravi replied.

"Which job?" Aditi replied, frowned, and started to munch again.

Ravi was taken aback. Then suddenly, Aditi asked, "Do you want a chapati?"

"No, I am done."

"I am still starving; let me order one. You know when you are sad, you feel like eating more," Aditi giggled and asked the waiter to get one chapati for her.

They were almost done when Ravi's phone buzzed. Ravi looked at his phone and frowned, "Ratan is back at the shop. We have to go".

They finished lunch, Aditi paid the bill and they walked to the car.

"Hey, thanks for lunch. I won't forget it," Ravi said.

"I like your company, Ravi. Will have lunch someday again," Aditi said and walked towards the car.

They drove back to the bank. Aditi parked the car and stepping out said to Ravi, "You sit in the car I will drop the cheque."

"No, it's okay. I will do it," Ravi replied.

"No, stay Ravi," Aditi instructed Ravi.

Ravi texted Ratan, "I will be there in 10 minutes. With Aditi now."

He looked at the message and then deleted the last line.

Aditi came back and said, "Let's go quick. I have a lot of work to do. One more thing, Ravi, what is your phone number? Sorry I didn't save it."

Ravi gave his phone number, and they drove back to the shop. Aditi dropped Ravi at the entrance of the lane.

When Ravi reached the shop, he saw Ratan standing near his bike. Ratan asked, "Who were you with?"

Ravi smiled and said, "With a friend," and walked inside the shop. Ratan followed.

"Where were you since morning?" Ravi asked.

"I had some personal work," Ratan said.

"Personal? What is so personal in your life that I don't know about," Ravi chuckled.

"Look at it in this way. It might be the same personal friend with whom you went for lunch," Ratan smiled.

Ravi ignored Ratan's comment and reminisced the moments spent with Aditi. Ratan too, was lost in his thoughts, trying to figure out who was in the abandoned house. How should he communicate with that unknown entity?

Suddenly Ratan asked, "Hey, did that girl come?"

"Girl, who?" Ravi asked.

"That girl who was supposed to pay us the money for the photography job for that haunted house," Ratan asked.

"Ratan, please, she has a name. *Aditi!*" Ravi grimaced.

"O Aditi fan! Did she come?" Ratan asked.

"Yeah, she came, gave the money. Don't worry," Ravi said.

"That's great. She paid the money too," Ratan said.

Ravi nodded his head.

"What happened to you? Since you are back from lunch, you are so quiet and lost," Ratan remarked.

"Nothing Ratan. Just leave me alone for a few minutes," Ravi replied with a silly grin.

"Did you go out with Aditi?"Ratan asked.

Ravi nodded again.

"No wonder you've been daydreaming. God help us!" Ratan shook his head in disappointment and sat near the counter.

"You should have looked at her today, Ratan. She was so bubbly," Ravi said, stretched on the chair and looking at the ceiling.

Ratan, while talking to Ravi, touched his pocket. It was the picture he had brought from that house.

"You know Ratan, she is an orphan. Sadly, she had to go through this so early in life," Ravi said, taking a deep breath.

"It's sad indeed. Did she tell you that?" Ratan asked.

"Yeah. But you know what, she has a short term memory. She forgets lots of things. She didn't even remember that we are helping her with the photography job," Ravi said. Ratan ignored what Ravi said and looked at the photograph.

Ravi asked, "Whose picture is that in your hand?"

Ratan slowly kept it in his pocket and said, "I will tell you soon. By the way, if she doesn't remember that we are assisting her with the job, does she remember that we have to go to the house tomorrow?"

"Oh yeah. I hope she remembers that," Ravi said and walked towards the counter where Ratan was standing.

"Ravi, do you believe in ghosts?" Ratan asked.

"After the visit to the house, frankly, I started to believe that ghosts exist," Ravi said.

"If you ask me, I am not convinced that there is a ghost in that house. But yes, at the same time, there is something wrong with that house," Ratan said.

"Don't think too much. We have that thread around our arms, nothing will happen to us. And we have not harmed anyone," Ravi said, taking a seat. Just then, Aditi called Ravi.

"What did she say?" Ratan asked.

"She said that instead of tomorrow, we will go on Saturday," Ravi said.

"Why?" Ratan asked.

"She is a busy girl. She was saying she has some other work that has come up. So I said that we are okay with Saturday."

Aditi hung up the phone after speaking with Ravi and went back to her desk. It was a busy day at the *Finite Times* office. Her boss called her up to cover an interview, even though she was on leave. She was not happy that she had to come to the office when she has taken the day off. While Aditi was at her chair, her subordinate walked past her desk with the report she had prepared.

Aditi looked at it and said, "What is this? The format of this report is so bad that I will not even look at it. Look at this picture. It should be in the center-left of the report. People will look at the content, and not that picture first. Please go now and fix it."

"Sorry, Aditi. I got it. Let me correct it," her subordinate said.

Everyone knew that Aditi wanted perfection in work. The staff said that she had learnt a lot from her mentor. She was very close to her. Aditi had no friends in the office. The only time she spoke to people was either for work or if she met someone at the coffee machine. She never went out for lunch with colleagues. The staff at Finite also looked at her as a loner.

One girl came to Aditi and said, "Boss is calling you."

Aditi shook her head, banged her hand on the desk with frustration, and went into Hari's cabin.

"Hey, Aditi! I am sorry, really sorry for calling you during your day off. Please have a seat," her Boss said.

"It's fine, boss, tell me when do I have to leave?" Aditi continued.

"This was one day I took off after so long. I have earned it, and you have snatched it from me. It's fine boss, tell me when do I have to leave," Aditi said in a low voice.

"You won't regret this interview, I promise. Remember you said that you would like to speak to Dr. Parichit Tripathi. Well, he is in town for the day and we got a slot for an hour. That hour is all yours girl. Go, get it."

Aditi crossed her arms and gave a tight-lipped smile.

Her boss found it strange that Aditi was not celebrating the news. He swiftly asked,

"What happened? I thought you would jump at this opportunity."

Aditi said, "Thank you, boss! Finally, he is here in town, great. It has been a long wait. When and where. Tell me, tell me, tell me," Aditi repeated.

"Now that is what I was looking for, be there at 7 pm sharp, Golden Gate hotel, just after his lecture," Hari replied.

"Thank you, boss. I will be there by 5," Aditi said.

When she was going out, Hari looked at her and said, "Aditi, wait. One minute."

"Yes, boss."

Hari kept his hand on her shoulder. "Aditi, you have to promise me that you will be patient with Dr. Parichit Tripathi. Don't boil up too soon."

"Yeah, I will. Sure."

"Aditi, listen. I know you very well. You have some notions about supernatural power. And Dr. Parichit Tripathi is the guru of Parapsychology sciences. He is not any local baba who became famous overnight. He has a wealth of knowledge, and people admire his thesis on supernatural powers, ghosts and psychology. You have to be respectful. You are taking Finite Times's reputation along with you. Don't let it get ruined," Hari said.

"I promise Hari, I know what you are saying," Aditi replied.

"Thanks. By the way, what assignment are you working on?" Hari asked.

"Ah, nothing serious. There is one simple story. I will wrap it up quickly," Aditi replied.

"Understood. Anyway, best of luck!" Hari said and saw Aditi walking out of the cabin.

Dr. Parichit Tripathi was well known for the research he had done on different subjects of human psychology, paranormal sciences, and parapsychology across the world. One of his famous papers, "Woman and Her Two Kids" was on the real-life story of a woman who had killed her two kids after being possessed by a demon in a small town in Texas. His write-up about the whole event and how the woman's brain functioned, what she was thinking, was researched so beautifully that it was cited in many other research papers and was awarded the best paper in the UK's annual psychology conference. Dr. Parichit Tripathi was a well-known name in the city.

Aditi had read a lot about him, and she had this perception in mind that whatever Dr. Parichit Tripathi does is not science but a hollow and baseless theory. The only point where she agreed with Parichit Tripathi was that ghosts don't exist.

In the office, no one knew why Aditi was so anxious to meet and interview him.

That evening at the Golden Gate Hotel, Aditi reached there around 6 pm. Dr. Parichit Tripathi was giving a lecture on parapsychology. So she sneaked in and got herself a place in the last row, corner seat where Dr. Parichit Tripathi couldn't see her.

Dr. Parichit was dressed like a sadhu. He wore three-four neckless of rudraksha beads lined up one after another around his neck. Three white parallel broad lines were drawn on his forehead. There was a red dot on the middle line.

He was almost wrapping up the session and about to open the forum for questions.

"As I explained in my session, a person suffering from Disassociated Identity Disorder, DID, may not be aware of other personalities inside them. They have memory loss which in medical terms is known as dissociative amnesia. You forget things like where you kept your spectacles when they're right there in your pocket. It's as if there are two people in a body, unaware of each other's existence. Parapsychology is a science that most scientists still try to correlate with a theory, but have not succeeded. There is a certain power that still can't be explained. Now let's open up the dais for the questions." One gentleman from the audience got up and asked, "Dr. have you conducted any experiment which can prove the existence of ghosts?"

"That's a good question. I want to stay with the fact that I have no evidence to confirm this. But yes, there is evidence to support this. You may call it circumstantial. Several journals have published their experiences that support these theories. So I won't say that paranormal doesn't exist," saying this the Dr. smiled and asked, "Any other questions in the house?"

A faint voice from the back asked, "What experiment have you conducted to prove that paranormal activity doesn't exist?"

"That's again a good question," he continued.

"If you are asking whether I have found something that I couldn't explain, yes, that's happened. There were 20 experiments tested among ten people. We did the regressive test, but it was inconclusive. We didn't find any evidence. That result was sent for validation, but it was quashed. God only knows why. That research received a lot of media coverage. However, since we were unable to convince them of the results, it was finally published in a local journal. I was getting questioned by the people who believed in paranormal activity, but I didn't get the point to prove them wrong. I was very hopeful that the paper that we were planning to publish would debunk some theories, but unfortunately, that didn't work out."

One member from the audience got up and asked, "Any such paranormal event that you would like to share, since you said in your response that you've tested the direct claim of paranormal activity?"

"You guys seem to have a strong belief in the existence of paranormal activity,"

Dr. Parichit chuckled and the audience also laughed with him. He waited for the crowd to settle, then continued, "Let me close this session by telling you about a letter that we received by a person who wanted us to investigate the happenings in her house. They said that they were not disturbed by its presence, and they wanted to stay in peace with whoever it was. So, here goes the letter.

Hi Doctor, I am Elene. We are a total of three occupants in the house. I have one grandmother who is in her late 80s, and a husky.

One day I helped my grandmother sit on the sofa. She cannot get up or sit without any support. To sit on the couch, she needs a pillow by her side to lean on. Her favourite TV show airs at 10 pm. That day she insisted on watching it sitting on the couch and not on the wheelchair. I sat near her, reading one book. After a while, the show finished, and I switched off the TV. She wanted to sleep on the couch itself so I removed all the cushions and kept them away. She dozed off within a few minutes. Our dog was lying down next to her sofa. The house was so quiet that even the sound of the pages flipping seemed loud. It was close to midnight. I could see the streetlight flickering outside the window.

Around midnight, my dog woke up suddenly and looked towards the kitchen. Then in a few seconds, he went rushing there. The dog reached the storeroom in the kitchen and started to sniff around. I am not sure how but the door of the storeroom opened slightly. My dog looked inside, and began to shiver. I looked towards the couch. My grandmother, who couldn't even sit without any support, was sitting up straight and looking towards the kitchen, eyes wide open. I was dumbstruck. I observed that the temperature of the room had suddenly dropped, and I started to feel cold. I rubbed my arms with my hands and began to breathe heavily. I got up from my sofa swiftly and asked my grandmother, "Anni, hey, what happened?"

She didn't move her head an inch and was constantly staring at the kitchen. I looked at my dog, who had now reached the couch. He seemed very normal, as if nothing had happened. Then I looked at my grandmother, and what shocked me was that she was lying down on the sofa. I am still baffled about what had happened. My heart was pounding loud enough for me to hear it.

The next morning, I asked my grandmother if she remembered what had happened last night. She spoke about how she had slept after the TV show was over. Similar incidents a few more times after this. I know someone is there in the house. But whoever it is, I am okay with it unless it harms us. I also don't want to disturb them and am okay to live peacefully."

Dr. Parichit took a pause and gazed around the auditorium. The audience was quiet. He started explaining.

"We did investigate the case. According to our findings, the three characters have individual behaviors, and after applying the parapsychology theory, they are attributed to independent responses. Overall, here paranormal science can't explain what it was. Elene's reaction was good that she was okay with whatever was happening in the house, and she thinks whoever they are should not be disturbed. This was the investigation on a direct claim Elene made, but we could not find enough evidence to prove that whatever was going on there, was something supernatural."

Aditi was listening to Dr. Parichit will rapt attention. She was glued to the way Dr. Parichit was putting up his points. Even though he was dressed up like a sadhu, his answers were very scientific and precise.

In a few minutes people got up from their seats and gave a standing ovation to Dr. Parichit. She also got up swiftly and sneaked out of the hall from the exit door. She walked to the reception and then to the blue lounge. There she waited for Dr. Parichit, where they were scheduled to meet for the interview.

6

You Saw Me, I was There

Aditi was sitting on the sofa waiting for Dr. Parichit's assistant to call her. She looked at the wall clock. It was 7:35 pm. He was late by 35 minutes. The wait for Dr. Parichit made her more anxious.

After a while, a lady walked into the room and said, Dr. Parichit is ready to meet you. He is sitting in the meeting room. He suggested that it would be a good place to have a conversation."

Aditi felt nervous. Finally, it was time. She stood up, ironed out a wrinkle on her dress using her hand, ran her hand through her hair. Then she picked up her iPad and moved towards the meeting room.

It was a big room. Dr. Parichit was seated at the far end, scribbling on his phone. He looked at Aditi and immediately stood up. He walked down to greet her with a smile on his face, extended his hand, and said, "Hello, Aditi!"

Aditi fumbled and said, "Hello, Dr. Parichit. How are you doing?"

She looked a little nervous.

Dr. Parichit said, "I am good. Come, have a seat. Would you like some water?" he asked as he handed over a glass of water to Aditi.

Aditi gulped the water, took a deep breath, and patted her wet lips using a tissue. She began to slowly relax and asked,

"How was your session?"

"It was good. A lot of interesting questions from the audience," Dr. Parichit said with a smile.

He leaned back in the chair and asked, "So, what do you want to know from me?"

Aditi said, "First of all, thank you for giving us time for this interview," she smiled and continued. "What would you like to tell those people who believe in the existence of paranormal activity and that spirits or ghosts exist? They have experienced some instances that can prove their existence. Isn't this against your theory?"

Aditi switched on the Voice Memos app to record the conversation. When Dr. Parichit started to speak, she leaned forward, an indication of how curious she was to listen to him.

"I always tell people that it's a science. There are some physical characteristics that can't be explained. But you don't have to be sceptical about it," Dr. Parichit said.

"So, there is no such thing as a ghost?" Aditi quickly asked.

"Yes, unless you make one up. It looks like you believe in ghosts," Dr. Parichit chuckled.

"No, no. I don't," Aditi replied.

"But you are convinced that people will believe in ghosts if you show them something like that?" Dr. Parichit asked.

"Yes, I think so."

Aditi looked at Dr. Parichit, then at the iPad. Within a split second, she looked at him again with the corner of her eye and smiled. This happened so fast that Dr. Parichit, who had been leaning against the chair, sat up straight and put his hand on his lips and looked at Aditi closely. He felt that he had said something which had triggered something in her to behave this way. Dr. Parichit was stunned to see the change in Aditi's body language.

"Do you sometimes feel that ghosts exist?" Dr. Parichit asked in a low voice.

"Yes," Aditi's said in a gravelly voice, giggled, coughed slightly, and adjusted her shoulder.

Dr. Parichit was taken aback at her response, but he tried not to show any reaction. He looked at Aditi with a poker face, "Have you ever seen a ghost? Or do you know anyone who has seen one?" Dr. Parichit asked.

"Yes, I know one place. But you can't go in there alone. Only I can take you there. She talks only to me."

Aditi leaned forward, spread her legs, kept both her hand on the legs and held the iPad with two fingers. There was a strange broad smile on her face.

"Who are you?" Dr. Parichit asked.

"Why should I tell you?" she spoke in a low raspy voice that sounded as if she had a sore throat.

"Where is Aditi? Who are you?" Dr. Parichit said in a commanding voice.

She laughed and then suddenly kept a finger on her lips, "Sssshhhhhh! Quiet! Let her take some rest. You don't believe in ghosts, now let me show you one."

She scratched her back and kept both her legs on a chair and sat in a squatting position, and kept on giggling while doing that.

"See, whoever you are, you are causing harm to her. She may be in deep pain, mentally. Leave her alone," Dr. Parichit begged her.

She laughed and kept her hand on her head. By doing this, she messed up all her hair. It became untidy and spread all over her face. She looked dreadful.

What Dr. Parichit was looking at was a psychological disorder. He knew what was happening in front of him.

Unknowingly, he had triggered something in her which made her change the way she was behaving. The girl who had come inside the room with a very submissive and calm aura had changed entirely. She was now squatting on the chair and growling at intervals. Her appearance was demonic. But for Dr. Parichit, it was a psychological disorder. Dr. Parichit decided to bring back Aditi very slowly. Without forcing the person to leave, he had to ask Aditi gently to come back. "I am sorry, I should not have said that I don't believe in ghosts. Please, can I speak to Aditi? I need to tell her that too," Dr. Parichit said as he took a deep breath.

"No! No! No!" Aditi shook her and continued in the same gravelly voice, "You preach to those simple-minded people in that room that we don't exist," she giggled and then shouted in a rough voice, slightly jumping on the chair.

"See, I died. Long back. But I can take control of anyone's body to tell people like you that we exist."

"Dead?" Dr. Parichit asked in surprise and questioned. He frowned and continued, "Then why did you choose Aditi's body. There are others also."

He looked at her and leaned forward to know the answer.

"Like you, she also doesn't believe in me. One day she walked into my house. She was looking for me, poor girl. And that's it. I liked the way she invited me to be inside her," Aditi said and giggled, and then she became sad.

"Do you and Aditi know each other?" Dr. Parichit asked.

Aditi nodded her head in agreement and made a crying face.

"Who are you? Can I help you in any way?" Dr. Parichit asked her.

She looked at Dr. Parichit and said, "Make her believe in ghosts. That is the only way she will listen to me. I want her to help me and understand my pain, what I went through and what I want," she said and made a crying face again.

"Okay, I will tell her. But unless you tell me your name, how can I tell her who came looking for her," Dr. Parichit asked.

She looked at Dr. Parichit, giggled, and gestured with her hand to bring his ear close to her.

Dr. Parichit has dealt with these kinds of cases before, so without hesitation, he leaned forward.

She leaned forward in that squatting position, eyes wide open, and whispered in his ear.

"She knows who I am. She is the one who called me to meet you." Aditi laughed and Dr. Parichit was terrified.

Dr. Parichit controlled himself and said, "See, I accept that ghosts exists. Please can you ask Aditi to speak to me, so I can tell her that?"

She giggled and said, "No! No! No!" and waved her index finger in front of him in disagreement.

"I am asking you to leave. I am here to meet Aditi; else I will leave the room," Dr. Parichit forced her to leave in a commanding voice.

Aditi stopped giggling.

She kept looking at him with a broad smile on her face, unblinking eyes, and her face turning blue slowly as if she was holding her breath.

Dr. Parichit kept waiting for Aditi to come back. He knew what Aditi was doing by holding her breath. He had faith that Aditi would come back. Suddenly the iPad slipped from her hand, and it fell with a loud sound. Aditi's entire body started shaking. She fainted and fell on the floor.

Dr. Parichit swiftly stood up and murmured, "Aditi, Aditi wake up!"

He quickly reached for a glass of water and sat near her. He put some water in his palm and was almost ready to sprinkle it on her face. She opened her eyes, gave a ghostly smile, and said, "Bye bye!" She closed her eyes again.

Dr. Parichit shouted, "Anybody here, come quick," and he sprinkled the water on her face. After a few minutes, Aditi came back and looked at Dr. Parichit.

"What am I doing on the floor? What happened to me? Water?" Aditi was baffled and looked at Dr. Parichit.

He smiled and said, "Nothing, Aditi. You fainted. It looks like you are too tired."

"Yeah, could be. I am sorry, Dr. Parichit." Aditi was quiet and looked around. After a few minutes, she said, "Please, let's continue our interview".

Dr. Parichit didn't want Aditi to realize what he had seen just a few minutes back. He said, "If you are feeling okay, let's continue."

"Thanks, doctor. Please let's finish the interview quickly. I am feeling tired, and I need some rest," Aditi said and sat on the chair.

Aditi spoke to Dr. Parichit for almost an hour. It went pretty normal and sober. There were instances where Dr. Parichit saw another personality emerging again. Still, he smartly suppressed the trigger.

Finally, the interview was over.

"Thanks, Dr. Parichit, it was an amazing interaction. I have wanted to chat with you for so long, and finally, I got the opportunity. You were fantastic. I will send you a final copy of our interview before sending it to print," Aditi smiled and turned to collect her things from the table.

Dr. Parichit felt she was uncomfortable as she was wrapping up. It might be because she had fainted. Dr. Parichit tapped her shoulder while she was collecting her things and said, "Don't worry about it, Aditi. Go home and take some rest."

Aditi suddenly paused and, without turning back, said in the same gravelly voice.

"You didn't tell her about me, huh!" She walked out of the room without looking at Dr. Parichit who stood there frozen, watching her go. Whoever the person was, had taken almost complete control of Aditi.

After a few minutes, one assistant came inside the meeting room. He saw Dr. Parichit sitting at the chair looking worried.

He went up to him and asked, "What happened to her? How was your interview? I hope all is well. We heard sounds of laughing and giggling coming out of the room."

"What happened was actually an interview of the interviewer. God bless her," Dr. Parichit gave an uneasy smile, shook his head in disappointment, stood up and walked out of the meeting room.

Aditi had left the meeting room feeling shameful about her having fainted in front of Dr. Parichit. She was tired, disoriented, with slightly telescopic vision, and confused while walking towards the parking. She stopped at multiple points and looked in the direction of her car. Once she reached her car, she sat there and felt like dozing off. Driving the car in such a condition could be risky. She had only one choice. She decided to call Ravi and request him if he could take her home.

She pulled the lever beside the driving seat to lean backwards. In that position she took out her phone and dialled Ravi's phone, "Hello Ravi, where are you?"

"Hey Aditi, we are here at our GB photo shop. Almost ready to close for the day. Tell me, how can I help you?" Aditi's soft voice was music to his ears.

"I need your help. Please can you drive me home? I am not feeling comfortable to drive back myself. I don't know what happened to me. A couple of hours back, I fainted during the interview. Somehow, I managed to finish it, but still, I don't feel confident enough to drive," Aditi requested.

"Oh, of course. I will be there right away. Just send me your location on WhatsApp," Ravi replied.

"Thanks Ravi!" Aditi sent the location to Ravi, hung up the phone and closed her eyes.

In the shop, Ratan looked at Ravi speaking over the phone and asked, "What happened to her now?"

"She is not feeling well, she fainted during the interview, and she wants me to drive her car and drop her home." Ravi smiled.

"Oh! Anyway, you are lucky. You got a new job. A chauffeur!" Ratan grinned and walked out of the shop holding the keys.

Ravi went to Ratan and kept a hand on his shoulder, "I can understand your pain. But don't feel sad, my friend. You will also meet the girl of your life one day."

Ratan shrugged off his hand and said, "I am happy to be alone. I don't want to be someone's chauffeur. You enjoy your drive with her. I will drop you there and then go home."

"But she said, she fainted. Till afternoon, everything was fine. Sometimes girls take things to heart. I am sure she must have discussed something in the interview which she would not have liked, and that's it. Poor girl, she works so hard. God knows what exactly happened," Ravi said while Ratan was closing down the shutter of the shop.

"That girl has given us a job. Think again; she is much smarter than both of us combined. There is something else going on. She might be having some physical problem, you know, blood pressure and all. God knows!" Ratan locked the shop and walked towards the bike.

"Hey, we both came separately today. You can go home. I will drive straight to this place, it's not that far, Golden Gate Hotel, near Bose Street. I will come back after dropping her home," Ravi said to Ratan.

"Okay, I will leave both of you alone," Ratan waved his hand and sat on his bike.

"See you tomorrow!" Ratan said.

Aditi had gone into deep sleep. When Ravi reached Golden Gate Hotel, he tried calling her from outside, but she didn't pick up the phone.

Golden Gate Hotel was just along the street, a standalone building with a significantly less open area between the main entrance and the reception. It had around 21 floors with a pool on top. Ravi entered the gate, and he parked his scooter at the side of the open space, which was already filled with many two-wheelers randomly lined up.

He went inside the hotel and asked the staff about the parking lot. They directed him towards the elevator, which went to the basement. Ravi took the lift to the basement. From the hotel's noisy reception to the silent parking floor, it was a dramatic change. While walking in the basement, there were patches of dark, just behind the tubelights and pillars. Even in that relatively small parking lot, it was tough for Ravi to find Aditi's car. He tried shouting Aditi's name, but it just echoed back. Ravi went to level one and then to level two. Meanwhile, he kept calling on her cell phone, but there was no response from her. After some time, Ravi found her car in basement two. It was parked on the corner most area of the floor. He knew the color of the car and some digits of the number plate, which helped him to locate it from afar.

He reached the car and looked inside. From a distance, it appeared that no one was there because Aditi had reclined her seat to sleep. As he reached closer, he looked inside the car and saw Aditi. The low light on her face made her look stunning as she slept. A car passed by and its headlights reflected on her face, which looked like a bright full moon that had just came out of the clouds for a few seconds. If given a chance, Ravi would have kept looking at Aditi throughout his life, standing there in the quiet basement.

Soon, the next car passed, and the light reflected on her face. This time he saw Aditi sitting upright on her seat, her eyes wide open. She was staring at him with her big eyes. Ravi was shocked to see that face. He went close to the car and slowly knocked on the driver seat window.

Aditi kept looking at him for a few minutes. Ravi knocked again and was surprised at why she was looking at him like that. He started to breathe fast, pulse accelerating, palms sweaty, and began to feel nervous looking at Aditi. Her beautiful face was replaced by a face with a dreadful stare, which was not romantic by any stretch of imagination.

After a few minutes, Aditi shook her head slightly, held her head with both hands as if she had a severe headache, and scrolled the window glass down. She looked at Ravi and said,

"Why are you staring at me? Can you drive the car?" Aditi asked.

Ravi nodded and just stood there.

"Okay then, please come in," Aditi shifted to the next seat, and Ravi sat on the driver's seat. Ravi's pulse gave no sign of settling down. He started the car, and kept quiet for some time so that he could feel normal.

"What happened to you?" Aditi asked.

Ravi was quiet and shook his head, indicating as if nothing had happened.

Aditi took out her phone and switched on the GPS, and marked her home location on it. Then slowly, she hooked it on the phone holder, which was mounted on the top of the car dashboard. She tilted the screen towards Ravi.

"I am sorry, Ravi, for calling you in urgency. I have a headache, and I have a feeling of vertigo often. And today, I fainted in front of Dr. Parichit. There is something happening to me. I need to see a doctor," Aditi said in a frustrating voice.

Ravi kept quiet and kept nodding his head slightly, indicating that he was listening to Aditi.

There was silence in the car. Only one voice was audible and that was Google assistant telling the direction to Aditi's home.

After a while, Aditi asked, "What happened to you? Why are you so quiet?"

Ravi shook his head again.

"You fought with Ratan?" Aditi frowned.

Ravi chuckled, "Not in this lifetime!"

"Oh, your bromance! Gosh. Then what happened? You have been quiet since you came," Aditi insisted.

Ravi took a deep breath and said, "Do you often make fun of people like that?

"First, I tried calling you almost a hundred times; you never picked up the phone. Then after that extensive search in the basement, I found your car. When I reached your car, and I saw you, you showed me that spooky, dreadful face. As if you were stunned to see me there. Then suddenly, you feel okay," Ravi said in an agitated voice.

"My phone? I am sorry, it must be on silent mode. While talking to Dr. Parichit, I must have kept it as is and not turned it off later. I am sorry for that," Aditi said submissively.

"And what about the expression on your face? As if you didn't recognize me," Ravi asked.

"Which expression? I must have woken up from a deep sleep. You were there, and I did recognize you," Aditi said.

Aditi observed that her headache was gone completely; there was no vertigo, no blurred or telescopic vision. As compared to what she was feeling a few hours ago, now all the pain was gone. What she couldn't remember was her conversation with Dr. Parichit just before she fainted. Thinking about all this, she looked alongside the road.

After some time, they reached the road. Cars occupied a quarter of the road parking on the sides.

"What's going on here?" Aditi said and looked around the cars.

"I have never seen such a crowd here."

"You don't know what's going on?" Ravi frowned.

"No!" Aditi replied.

"It's the temple of goddess Kali. Today is the Mahakali Jayanti. This day is the most auspicious day to worship Maa Kali. This day is to banish the negativity surrounding us. People visit this temple, most of the time, who are possessed by spirits. They come here to get themselves free of them," Ravi said.

Aditi, while listening to Ravi, looked at the string lights overhead that made it look like they are driving under the blanket of twinkling lights or a glittering tunnel. She could see the series of twinkling lights of different shapes and colors hanging on the streetlight poles. She was mesmerized and the beauty gave her a sense of calmness. Ravi saw the twinkling lights reflecting in her shiny eyes. Her face glowed under those orange street lights.

Ravi slowed the car down; it was a treat to see her smiling. Aditi looked so beautiful under those twinkling lights that if Ravi were to die in the next five minutes, it would be his last wish to keep looking at Aditi.

Ravi asked in a low voice, "Do you want to stop and have a look at the temple? If you are not tired?"

Suddenly Google Assistant said, "Continue straight for one kilometer and then turn right".

Aditi looked at Ravi and then at the phone and chuckled.

"Yeah, let's go. I am feeling much better now. At least inside the temple, I will find more peace."

Ravi parked the car on the side, and both of them got down from the vehicle. He took out his phone and texted something to Ratan.

After walking around a few hundred meters, they reached the temple. The path till the temple gate was quiet. When they reached the gate, the loudspeaker on the main entrance was amplifying the song which the ladies inside the temple were singing. They both walked inside the temple.

Ravi said curiously and in a loud voice, "You may not like this place, especially since it's said that people who are possessed or have spiritual afflictions come here for treatment. You don't believe in ghosts, right?"

Aditi gave a slight shake of her head and stopped while Ravi kept walking.

After a few minutes, when he didn't hear anything from Aditi, he looked beside him. He was surprised to see that Aditi was not around. He scanned through the crowd in the temple, but there was no sign of her. She had vanished into thin air.

7
Peek-a-boo

After Ravi had gone to meet Aditi, Ratan stood at the G.B. photo Studio thinking about the house. He kept thinking about the voice he had heard when he was there in the room. And what about that door which was locked from inside? Surely, something was not right in there. He decided that he would go to Saleem uncle's stall and think about what to do next. Ratan drove his bike and reached Saleem uncle's stall. As usual, Saleem uncle was busy with the customers. His stall was like a beehive; the way customers surrounded the stall amazed Ratan as they couldn't even get ten percent of the footfall in their shop.

"Sometimes, I feel Ravi is right. We should close G.B. photo Studio and open a grocery store. At least we will have some crowd in the shop then, he thought and pulled a chair, sitting there thinking about the house. It had become a big mystery for him. Whenever he thought about the house, he was faced with a host of unanswered questions. While he was deep into that thought, someone tapped his shoulder. Startled, Ratan looked behind. It was Saleem uncle.

"You scared the hell out of me, uncle," Ratan said.

"An agitated mind is like muddy water; you can't see clearly. You have to wait for it to settle down and then find what you are looking for," Saleem uncle said.

"But what if the mystery keeps on growing dark and deep? It baffles you day and night. It doesn't let you sleep, eat, or drink. It's everywhere! What should I do?" Ratan asked, disturbed.

"You have two ways to handle this. Either solve it and get the answer or find another big mystery. The new mystery will override the previous one. But that is not a good way to overcome a problem. The best option would be to solve the mystery itself," Saleem uncle smiled.

Ratan took a deep breath and poured himself a glass of water.

"See Ratan; I told you even that day. Take money from me. Pay me later, but you wanted to tackle the situation yourself," Saleem uncle said.

"It's not about that Saleem uncle. We got the money. That problem is solved, Aditi helped us with that cheque against the job," Ratan said.

"That's good news. Then what is bothering you so much?" Saleem uncle asked.

"It's just that..." Ratan paused and said, "Nothing, uncle. Nothing".

Saleem uncle said, "If you have committed to Aditi to finish the job, then you have to do it. This is how you keep promises in business, and I don't have to tell you that. But always remember, your job is just to finish the given task. Why, who, or what is not your problem."

"Thanks uncle. I think it's better that I finish the job and get done with it," Ratan said.

Saleem uncle brought out two plates of pav bhaji for both of them.

"You know Ratan, that thread that I tied around your arm, don't ever take it off. It will protect you from all the evil forces and ill thoughts,"Saleem uncle said while eating the pav bhaji and continued, "Once you start believing something to be true or real, your mind will then be conditioned to believe it to be true, even if it isn't. This will trigger a chain of thoughts that will develop anxiety and anxiousness, and ultimately, it will keep eating you from the inside."

"Thanks uncle. God knows why, but since I have visited that house, thoughts keep coming from all directions that there is something that I need to find out. There is something, something inside the house which is calling me." Ratan made a fist and punched in the air to express his desperation.

"Do you believe in ghosts?" Saleem uncle asked.

"No! Never!" Ratan said.

"Then there is nothing in that house," Saleem uncle said, but Ratan countered.

"No uncle, there is something in that house," he said.

Saleem uncle looked at him and replied, "Then go discover it!"

Ratan became quiet and started to eat.

"What happened? You don't want to go? You don't want to find out?" Saleem uncle asked curiously.

Ratan paused and said, "Yes, I want to find it. But I don't want Ravi to know about it."

"What? Why?" Saleem uncle was baffled.

"I don't have an answer for that, uncle. I am only following what my heart is telling me to do right now," Ratan replied.

"Only thing I can say is, please keep yourself safe. Whatever you do, if you keep Ravi along, he will only be of help to you. Two heads are always better than one," Saleem uncle said.

Ratan thought, *"The other head is following Aditi nowadays,"* and smiled.

"What happened? Why are you smiling?" Saleem uncle asked.

"Nothing uncle. Nothing, "Ratan replied and finished the pav bhaji. They sat there for a few minutes talking.

After speaking to Saleem uncle, Ratan was firm in his decision of going again in the house to find out the truth. He wanted to solve the mystery.

"Thanks Saleem uncle for your company. It is always great talking to you. Now unless I find the answers, I won't settle down. But please don't let Ravi know about it," Ratan requested him.

"It's hard to keep a secret from you two. I would always like that both of you stay together and always help each other. I would still say, take him along. He will only be of help," Saleem uncle advised Ratan.

"I have never hidden anything from him, Saleem uncle. But this is not the right time. Probably he will not understand me now. But soon, I will explain everything to him," Ratan smiled.

"And do take care of that thread. It will take care of you both," Saleem uncle said pointing at his arm.

"Absolutely uncle," Ratan said goodbye to Saleem uncle and drove his bike towards the house 666/13B.

Saleem didn't have a good feeling about the house. Since Aditi had told them the story, Saleem had felt that he should tell Ratan and Ravi not to take this job. But he wanted the boys to make their own decisions.

After half an hour, Ratan reached the house. It was around 8 pm and it was pitch dark. The only street light was a mix of yellow and orange, shining dimly on the house. He switched off the engine. The crazy guy who was sitting outside of the house was still there, sleeping with a blanket over him. It was quite strange for Ratan to see someone in that lone house. Apart from the rustling of the Ashoka trees, he could hear the faint sound of hymns coming from the Kali temple, which was not far from that house. The only light on the façade was from the streetlight. The house was completely dark. After hiding his bike among the Ashoka tress, he walked on the path covered with gravel, leading to the main door. He looked up and saw that the ripped curtains were blowing due to the wind from the window cracks. He remembered that he had seen someone's head peeping through the same window. Ratan walked in, determined to uncover the mystery and possibly, also debunk the myth of spirits or ghosts in the house. While he was walking on the path, he heard something behind him.

He swiftly turned around. There was nothing, no one.

"It might be some insects making that sound," Ratan said to himself and started to walk again towards the door. His pulse started to accelerate, but he took deep breaths to keep himself calm.

After a few minutes, he reached the door and extended his hand towards the knob, but the door squeaked open. Ratan was taken aback. He waited there at the door and gave himself a pep talk.

"See Ratan, if you want to know what is inside, you have to go in. Period!" Ratan stood there for a while, touched the thread on his arm, said a silent prayer, and then stepped in.

He turned on the torchlight on his phone and scanned around. He looked around the hall and saw a tiny portion of street light coming inside the room through the cracks of the window, along with the sound of rattling leaves and hymns from the temple. Every time Ratan looked into the dark patches, it made him feel that someone was standing there, but when he flashed the torchlight into the dark, there was no one.

The sound of his phone beeping startled him and he almost jumped. He had a WhatsApp notification from Ravi. He swiped it to read,

"I am outside the Kali temple with Aditi. My battery is low, in case it gets discharged and mummy calls, please tell her that I will be late tonight. Please (a smiley with folded hands)."

Ratan shook his head and replied to Ravi, "Okay sir," and murmured,

"This girl will take him for a ride one day."

He kept the phone back in his pocket and stood there. He was thinking of walking up the stairs. He heard a thud of a footsteps as if someone was running upstairs. Ratan's pulse was accelerating, and heart pounding. In a few minutes, there was sweat on his forehead and his palms. He touched his forehead which felt moist. He gathered all his strength and decided to take the stairs. He took slow steps and started to climb up. He could hear someone giggling and whispering faintly in the room. Ratan kept looking upwards while taking the steps. When he had crossed the halfway mark, he saw a light coming from the room. The same blue colored room which Ramchandani had built in anticipation of a baby boy. Ratan saw a shadow, as if someone was sitting on the floor and scribbling something. He took a few steps looking upwards, but tripped.

The shadow in the room was now still.

A voice from the room said, "Mummy, is it you?" and giggled.

Voices in the deathly silence terrified Ratan. His heart pounded and palm was wet with sweat. He was clearly shaken. From the sound, Ratan guessed it was the voice of a girl in her teens. He swiftly stood up, tip-toed close to the passage wall.

The girl asked again, "Mummy?"

There was dead silence. Ratan held his breath. He started to move slowly towards the room. The door closed with a loud sound. Ratan stood there for around half an hour, expecting the door to open. Ratan prayed hard that he would get a chance to talk to her. But she remained inside. It was astonishing to think that someone in this haunted house would stay alone. But she was not alone, she had her mummy too. Were they hiding from someone? Were they criminals? Or was it a spirit who was playing and didn't want to reveal its identity to the outside world.

Thinking about all this, Ratan reached the door and tried to open the doorknob. There was a sound of the click, and it opened. The door was not locked; it was just shut. He opened the door slightly. There was no one. He was shocked to see that there was no one inside the room.

He looked all over, behind the door, in the wardrobe, outside the window. The girl was gone without a trace. It was hard to believe that someone could disappear from a closed room. He was on the verge of agreeing that someone only with supernatural powers could do this. This might be a ghost. His heart was pounding and screaming that it's a ghost, but his mind was adamant that it's a human.

Ratan was puzzled, surprised and lost in unanswered thoughts. He walked and stood at the gallery—looking at the long Ashoka trees in the dark. While he was deciding what to do next, he felt someone silently creeping up behind him. He was frozen for a few seconds, then swiftly turned back. Again, there was nothing. A gust of air came in. The disappearance of the girl and the sudden gust of air were signs that things were not normal here. He was standing with all these thoughts surrounding him, when he heard the sound of gravel being crushed on the pathway with heavy footsteps, as if someone was walking on it quickly. Ratan went to the pink room, which faced the house entrance, and peeped outside to see. He felt that someone had just entered through the main door and got inside the house. In the dim light, all he could make out was that it was someone with long hair and a slim body, wearing a jacket and heavy shoes. He pulled out the phone from his pocket to switch on the torch.

He slowly went to the passage and peeped. He saw a girl close the door, take off her shoes. For a split second, the light from the window cast a glow on the girl's face.

Ratan was stunned. It was Aditi!

He couldn't believe what he just saw. A few minutes back, he had received a message from Ravi that Aditi was with him. Then who was this girl?

Taking out her shoes, the girl silently went towards the kitchen and then to the storeroom adjacent to it. She opened the door, went inside the room, and closed the door.

Ratan swiftly went downstairs. He kept his ears on the door and tried hard to listen to what was going on, but there was dead silence. He was frustrated with how people disappeared within seconds in this house. It was driving him crazy.

He slowly opened the door and saw a flight of stairs going down. He could only see a few steps with his torchlight. He followed the stairs and reached the storeroom. There were only a few things scattered in the storeroom and it was quite empty otherwise. He looked around, and found no one. In the storeroom, he saw one switch. He tried his luck and switched it on. A bulb switched on. The only way he knew someone could disappear from the room was if there was a door to exit. While he searched, he could also hear someone else's footsteps in the room, along with his. He could sense someone moving behind him. Ratan quickly ran towards the light and turned around; there was a girl standing in the shadow, facing him.

He shouted, "Who are you?"

The girl didn't move but started to make a growling sound.

Ratan once again asked her, but her growling became louder and louder.

Ratan shouted in a commanding voice, "Whoever is there come out! If you have guts, show me your face!"

The growling stopped.

"Why did you come here?" the girl asked him. She stepped into the light. Now her face was clearly visible.

"Aditi!" Ratan shouted and froze in shock.

Aditi's appearance had changed completely. She smirked at him, her lank hair partly covering her face. Her eyes wide open, flamed with hatred. It was evident that she did not want Ratan there.

"What you are doing in this house now?" Ratan asked.

She suddenly burst into maniacal laughter. Then suddenly she stopped and stared at him with an angry face, "This is my house!"

Ratan was surprised to hear that, and he asked, "Your house?" He asked, "Who is that girl?"

"What girl?"

"That girl in the room upstairs."

Aditi was surprised. It was as if Ratan had asked her something which was a secret and only she knew about it.

"She is my daughter," she said and giggled.

Since the beginning, Ratan was not ready to believe that something paranormal was happening in the house. But now he had been presented with a clear piece of evidence. Aditi did not look or talk like a normal person. She appeared to be possessed.

"What? Your daughter?" Ratan kept his hand on his head and knelt on the ground.

"But…" Ratan said. Before he could continue, Aditi held one leg of a heavy square shaped coffee table with one hand, and threw it towards him. Ratan tried to dodge it, but the edge of the table struck his head extremely hard. There was a big thud.

Ratan fell flat on the floor. He saw Aditi run away from that spot like a thief running away from a house after being seen. While climbing the stairs, she stumbled, got up and started to limp while climbing up. This was the last thing that Ratan saw before he became unconscious.

In the Kali temple, Ravi was frantically looking for Aditi. He searched for her in every nook-and-corner of the temple. Ravi was stuck in the sea of crowd. Ravi stood there for an hour, till the arti finished, in anticipation that he would spot Aditi. He knew calling Aditi on her phone was of no use in that crowd.

After the arti got over, the crowd broke away from the front like a sea of people. Ravi couldn't go ahead as he had to go with the flow to come out. He kept calling out Aditi's name, but with no result. It had been almost two hours.

He dialled her phone and waited for her to pick it up, but she didn't respond. Frustrated, Ravi kept dialling her number back-to-back, but it was of no use. Feeling helpless, he walked out of the temple and reached the car. He opened the car door and sat on the driving seat. It was very late, ten minutes past midnight. Looking at his battery power at 1%, he texted his mother that he will come late today.

Later, he said to himself, "Where are you, Aditi? Why are you playing Peek-a-boo?"

Ravi was tired and baffled by Aditi's behaviour. He closed his eyes and remembered all the moments he had spent with Aditi that day. In a few minutes, he saw Aditi walking towards him. She opened the car door, and quietly sat beside him. She looked dazzling in that beautiful red dress. She looked at Ravi with a mesmerizing smile. The smile which could heal a million wounds. The smile that could bring the smell of rain in a hot desert. The smile could make a dead man smile. A smile worth dying for a million times. It was hard to take his eyes away from her. Aditi started to talk and smile, and so did Ravi. They kept talking and laughing. A car honked sharply. Ravi opened his eyes and rolled down the car window. He was shocked. It was morning, and it made him realize that he had fallen asleep in the car. He looked to the side. He dialled her number. There was a vibrating sound in the car.

"Oh, no, not again, Aditi. You forgot your phone in the car," Ravi said.

He looked at the back of the car. Aditi was sleeping like a log in the back seat.

Ravi smiled and said, "Aditi, Aditi. Wake up!"

She didn't move. Ravi shook her slightly and tried to wake her up. It felt like she was having a sound sleep after a long time.

Ravi took some water in his hand and splashed on her face. Aditi woke up and looked at Ravi.

"Hey, it's morning!" she said, surprised.

"Yes, it is," Ravi said, nodding his head and continued.

"Where were you the whole night? You had disappeared from the temple. I kept looking for you."

"I don't know what happened Ravi," Aditi sat down, rubbed her eyes, yawned and continued,

"I was walking beside you, and suddenly that headache struck again. It was sharp; I sat near the bench. Then someone took me to the side and made me sit there to watch these women who were waving and shaking their heads in the air. It was so annoying. Then, I looked for you; you were gone. I had no option but to come out of the temple. Then I thought to take some medicine, so I went to this medical store. There I took some aspirin, came back and sat in the car. After a few minutes, I fell asleep. When I woke up, I saw you were sleeping, smiling and talking to yourself. It was funny to watch you," Aditi chuckled and continued. "I kept asking you and shook you also, but you were in a deep sleep. I thought there was no use talking to you and slept on the back seat."

Ravi blushed as he remembered his dream.

Ravi asked, "You were talking to me. Really?"

"Of course I was talking to you!" Aditi replied.

"Let me drop you home," Ravi said and asked her to come to the front seat.

Aditi came out and sat on the front seat. Ravi looked at her. He smiled and remembered his dream where he was talking to her.

"What happened to you?" Aditi frowned.

"Nothing" Ravi started the car and switched on Google navigation.

Aditi swiftly switched it off and said, "I will guide you."

Ravi drove the car slowly out of the temple lane, when his phone rang.

'Ratan's Mummy' popped up on the phone.

Ravi smiled and picked up the phone. He stopped the car on the side.

"Hello Aunty!"

"Ravi, where are you? What happened yesterday? Ratan was not home the whole night. He has a bandage on his head. He is saying there are some stitches. What happened? Tell me the truth. Did you guys fight with someone? Tell me Ravi," Ratan's mummy was speaking loudly enough for Aditi to hear her voice clearly.

Ravi said, "Don't worry Aunty. I will be there in sometime," and he hung up.

"What happened to Ratan?" Aditi asked.

"He was fine till I left him at the shop. We also told those loan sharks that we will pay the installment. What could have happened to him?" he paused.

"Only Ratan can tell me what exactly happened."

Ravi was worried.

Aditi told Ravi, "You sit. I will drive today and drop you home."

Ravi nodded his head.

Aditi added, "Also, I will go and see a doctor today. This is very annoying."

"Shall I come with you? If you don't mind," Ravi asked.

"For now I would say Ratan needs you more than me. Stay with him," she kept her hand on Ravi's hand and continued, "You have helped me a lot since yesterday. Go stay with him. If I need any help, I will call you."

Ravi guided Aditi to reach Ratan's house.

"Do you want to come in?" Ravi asked Aditi.

"No, it's fine. He is sleeping anyway. I will meet him later," Aditi replied.

"Okay then. See you. Goodbye," Ravi said.

"Yeah, goodbye!" Aditi replied.

Ravi rang the bell.

Aunty opened the door, looked at Ravi, and started gently weeping.

"What happened aunty? Is Ratan okay?"

Aunty pointed upstairs. Ravi went flying to his room. He reached and slowly peeked inside.

Ratan covered his head with his hand and said, "Come inside. Nothing has happened to me. I am alive," Ratan replied.

Ravi took a deep breath and asked, "So what happened?"

Ratan slowly stopped laughing and became quiet. Nothing, I fell from the bike.

Ravi looked at him with pursed lips and a questioning face. He was not convinced with his response.

"Fell from the bike? Okay. Where were you all night?" Ravi questioned Ratan.

"In the hospital," Ratan quickly replied as if he was ready with that answer.

"Hospital?" Ravi repeated and continued. "Okay, and you didn't call me? Once?"

"You were with Aditi, so I didn't want to disturb you," Ratan replied.

"But you could have at least called me!" Ravi said angrily.

Ratan said, "Leave it, Ravi. Now you are enquiring like my mummy. I am okay, doesn't that make you happy?

"Tell me, how is Aditi? By the way, when did you drop her home?"

"Just now," Ravi replied.

"What! Just now? Are you serious?" Ratan asked shocked, and continued, "What were you guys doing all night?"

Ravi said, "Nothing, Ratan, I was sleeping on the front seat, and she was at the back seat of the car. It's a long story. I will tell you later. Leave it."

He looked at Ratan's bandage and said, "Do you want to go to the doctor again?"

"No need! He said I need to rest for at least 1-2 days. After that, I will be fine. He will take out the stitches later. There are only a few," Ratan said.

"Okay then. You stay here. I will go home and take some rest. I didn't sleep well yesterday night. I will drop by in the afternoon again," Ravi said and started to walk out of the room.

"Hey Ravi," Ratan stopped Ravi when he was walking.

"Will you tell me one thing? Honestly?" Ratan looked at Ravi and asked.

"Yeah, tell me?" Ravi said.

"Aditi was with you the whole night?" Ratan asked.

Ravi blushed and then chuckled, "Yeah."

"Can you do a favor for me? Without letting her know that I asked about her, please check if she has any twin sister. I mean her look-alike," Ratan asked.

"You need sound sleep Ratan. It looks like you seriously need some rest. And I don't have to ask her that. She is the only child to her parents. Leave her alone!" Ravi replied, shaking his head in disapproval.

"Okay, understood. I won't ask. Now take rest," Ratan said.

Ravi shrugged his shoulders.

"Okay then, goodbye. You too, sleep well," and Ravi left for his home.

While coming out of Ratan's house, he looked at his motorbike. He thought of having a look at it, where exactly it was damaged because of the accident. He stood there and looked at it very closely. There was not a single scratch or dent. Ravi shook his head in disappointment.

"Idiot! Can't even make up a good story. At least learn how to lie, Ratan Gandhi!"

8
Hunt for the Heart

It all started in Ajay's childhood. His mother and father did everything to bring them out of poverty, but it didn't happen till Ajay became a surgeon at Gangaram, which helped his family really pull them out of dearth. His mother still believed it was not just Ajay's hard work but also what the tantric directed to them to do as a part of rituals to feed and please Kaal. She used to tell Ajay about the story of the tantric and his supernatural powers. She convinced Ajay that he should not forget to please Kaal till he is alive. Ajay had been so strongly brainwashed since he was a child that even when he grew up to be a surgeon, he believed in what his mother had said about Kaal. One day when he was in his teens, he asked his mother.

"Maa, what does Kaal look like? Is he a human, a saint? Can we meet Kaal one day?"

"Kaal is everywhere, Ajay. He keeps watching us, he protects us. He will bring abundant joy and money in your life if you keep him happy. The tantric knows how to do so. He is always guiding us," his mother said and took out a picture of a creature engraved on a copper plate, which had the lower half of a man's body and the upper half of a bat with large horns jutting out of his head. It had wings spread wide, teeth visible because of a scary smile, and big eyes. She continued,

"One day, when the tantric was in our village, I asked him about Kaal. Seeing my eagerness, he gave me this plate. Look at it. You know that the tantric is blind since birth. In the place of his eyes, the tantric has skin all over, no eyes. People say he was born like that because Kaal wanted him to be like that. Kaal wanted the tantric to see people using his ears, like a bat. Kaal only communicates with the tantric in this physical world and no one else. This copper image has been created by the tantric with his nails. Can you believe it? Being blind, how can some make such a beautiful image? Unless he has some supernatural powers," she said as she handed over the copper plate to Ajay.

Ajay's mother opened a book covered with black cloth. She handed that too to Ajay.

"Ajay, this is Akalkhand. All the rituals here are mentioned in detail on how you can complete these steps, what is required, that can help you to please Kaal and reach Moksha. At the end of the book, it teaches you how to communicate with the dead and bring them back if you master some skills. Today, I am giving this to you. Whenever you think that you need Kaal's help, you can find your way through this book."

Ajay took that copper plate and looked at it very closely. The image outline was done with such precision that an experienced artist would need a specific instrument to create it. That image was engraved in Ajay's mind as Kaal, forever.

The death of Ajay's father was a mystery. There was a rumor in the village that Ajay's mother had sacrificed Ajay's father to bring them out of poverty, in consultation with the tantric. Ajay didn't believe that. His love for his mother remained untainted. His belief in the tantric and Kaal was well established because of his mother.

While at Gangaram, when he was sent on the assignment to Bastar, he knew that he would have to come back soon. He was unsure whether Manju could continue the rituals they had started together to reach Moksha, and if Kaal would be happy with it. Lately, Manju was not comfortable with the things she was doing. He remembered one day when he was leaving for Bastar, he had spoken to Manju in his cabin.

"I convinced Dr. Mitra, but he is adamant. I won't be around Manju, but you know what to do with that patient in my absence, right? When you take out the kidney, remember that you have to chant the mantra. Kaal will be waiting and watching for your sacrifice," Ajay said.

"But Ajay, she doesn't have any complications related to chronic kidney disease (CKD). You know all the tests were negative. It's working fine. I told you last time, Ajay I will only support you when the hospital has lost all hope to bring that organ back to life," Manju insisted.

"This is important for our life. We can't stay together if we don't complete these rituals and don't make Kaal happy. You know we are only a few steps away. I told you what Akalkhand says if we want to live beyond this lifetime, talk to spirits to help others, reach Moksha. You will have to complete these rituals. We need her kidney to be sacrificed. I don't want to lose you, Manju. Just think once again if we have the power to speak with the dead, how much help we can be to the others!" Ajay said.

"I think I should not believe you, Ajay. Enough of this now. My sister discovered that book you gave to me, and she now knows that I am involved in these practices. We had a big argument, which is something that has never happened before. In the hospital, too, people are making up stories. It's just because they have faith in my ability as a surgeon that the hospital management hasn't thrown me out. You go to Bastar Ajay; I will re-think about all this and then decide if I should continue with these rituals," Manju said and walked out of Ajay's cabin.

Ajay was not happy with what Manju had said. He left for Bastar the next day. Back at Gangaram, Manju was caught when she tried to steal a healthy organ from a patient, her kidney. Ramchandani saved her, else the management was ready to report this incident to the police and put Manju behind bars. But saving Manju from the arrest came with a premium that Manju would have to marry Ram. Ram was in love with her. Ram knew Manju was not a monster, but needed to believe that love didn't need any rituals and sacrifice. Ram had a firm belief that Manju would be fine with his true love. Fearing arrest, Manju didn't have a choice but to marry Ram. Ajay got the news of their marriage a week after he reached Bastar. He never called up Manju, and he continued the rituals to please Kaal more voraciously. Ajay was pained, but he didn't want to give up because he had transformed his pain to be his strength. Ajay went into deep meditation and performing sacrifices.

During his meditation, he was never able to meet the tantric. He yearned to meet him and be one of his disciples. He was convinced that he was not able to meet him because he had not done enough. Even during his meditation, Ajay never forgot Manju. She always hovered in his thoughts. This was one of the reasons that even after years of meditation, Ajay had never achieved what he had wanted. In this frustration, Ajay decided that he would meet Manju and try to bring her back to stay with him. Without her with him, it wasn't possible for him to focus on his meditation. So now, Ajay decided that he would meet Manju and somehow convince her to come back.

Ram's business was not doing well. They had a daughter, Hema, who was suffering from severe mental illness, earlier detected as ADHD but which was actually schizophrenia. Many years later, Ajay came back to Manju. The love Ajay carried for Manju was untouched. Manju had tried hard to wipe Ajay from her thoughts and memory. But as soon as she set eyes on him, every moment that she had spent with Ajay came rushing back.

"I tried to forget you, Manju, but it didn't happen. You are everywhere. I can't achieve what I want to, without you. So please, I beg you to come back with me," Ajay pleaded.

"Ajay!"Manju shouted and continued, "I left that life long back. I have moved on, and you should too. There is nothing in pleasing Kaal or achieving Moksha. Kaal and Moksha are all fiction; they don't exist. Look around us; we need to be with our people. So please leave that Ajay, for god's sake."

There was nothing in the world that could convince Ajay.

"Kaal will unite us back Manju. He is looking at us; he is looking at you. He wants you to come back and stay with me. See what happened around you. Ram is going through a lot of trouble. Hema is not normal. This has happened to you because you left the rituals in between. You have deceived Kaal, you insulted him. If you want Hema to be cured or Ram to be prosperous again, then you have to come back with me," Ajay said.

"If this is my destiny, then let it be. I will always be with Ram and Hema, no matter what. And your Kaal won't do any harm to us. Frankly, Ajay, look around. He doesn't even exist. It's all made up. Your mother lied to you," Manju said.

Ajay was not ready to listen to anything against Kaal or his mother. That was like pouring molten iron in his ears.

"Enough of this Manju. If you want to stay under the curse of Kaal, then so be it. But before I leave, let me warn you. Kaal is watching you and your family. If you can't be mine, then you don't have any right to live. He will curse you," Ajay got up, blew a powder-like substance around the room, and said, "Goodbye Manju!"

Manju smiled and said, "This is all a sham! Let me see who wins… Kaal or my faith in god."

Ajay left Manju's house in anger.

The next day, Manju and Ram were found dead in the house. Ajay had never left the city. When he heard that Manju and Ram were dead, he wanted Manju's dead body in his custody. He wanted to meet the tantric to bring her back, and this time when Manju would be back, she would be his. Because her soul would be in Ajay's debt forever.

Ajay opened the Akalkhand. According to the rituals written in Akalkhand, Ajay needed to get Manju's body within two days of her soul leaving the body. After that, Ajay wouldn't be able to bring Manju back to life. This was a challenge for Ajay because the deaths had taken place under mysterious circumstances and police had taken their bodies into custody. Manju's sister had taken Hema with her, but her behavior had become very violent as she couldn't find her parents around. Ragini admitted her to the hospital for special care. It was hard to keep her in the house.

Hema was admitted to the hospital. A few days later, one girl in her late twenties was also admitted to the same hospital. It was a case of trauma where the patient was raped and almost left for dead. She survived, but it was a typical case of Post-traumatic stress disorder (PTSD).

When doctors tried to get her to speak. But even after a month, there was no reply from her. She had vivid nightmares; a reminder of the trauma she had undergone.

Most of the time, she was quiet and unmoving, sitting on the bed. Just next to her was Hema. As a standard practice, Hema was kept tied up with straps. But lately, Hema had begun to show improvement. She was calmer and less violent than when she was first brought there by Ragini. One day the rape survivor saw Hema sitting quietly. Hema looked innocent, in her early teens. That face and innocence made her talk. She went to her bed and touched her hand; Hema looked at her and smiled.

"How are you feeling now?" the girl asked.

Hema nodded her head. She was quiet, afraid, and a little shy.

"Don't be afraid. I am your friend. You are Hema, right?"

She nodded again.

The girl smiled and said, "My name is Aditi."

Aditi had gone through the worst in her life. Hema was like the sunshine of summer in her life after a long gloomy winter.

Meanwhile, Ajay had managed to bribe the hospital staff and steal Manju's body from the mortuary. But he was late; it had been three days since her death. Ajay decided to carry out the final rituals and keep Manju's ashes with him. One day, when he would attain Moksha and get the power to speak to the dead, he would bring Manju back.

When Ajay read the Akalkhand, he realized that to bring back Manju, he needed to sacrifice a human connected to Manju, who shared her blood. The most important organ for the ritual was the heart. Finding Hema's heart now became his only purpose in life.

In the mental hospital, Aditi became close to Hema. For Aditi, Hema was a reason to live now. Both Hema and Aditi were orphans. This was one of the reasons Aditi shared a strong bond with Hema. Aditi decided that when she would be discharged from the hospital, she would also take Hema along. But that was not expected to happen soon. Hema had mental issues since childhood, so her recovery was not that fast. Aditi had to wait till Hema recovered fully.

Aditi was discharged from the hospital. Soon after discharge, she found a job as a journalist. She kept in touch with Hema. In her office, Aditi met her mentor Ragini Iyer, who was about to retire. She was a big helping hand to Aditi and much more than a mentor.

Ajay began his search for Hema. He shifted to the city permanently and found one secluded area, away from the city chaos. This house was apt for carrying out the rituals required for Kaal, located in the corner of the lane. The initial information he got was that Hema had left with her aunt, Ragini, after Manju had died. Ajay had never met Ragini and only heard her name from Manju when they were together. Now he got to know that Ragini was working in the same city with a magazine company.

One day Ajay decided to meet Ragini in her office to know where Hema was. Ragini was about to retire, so she was not allocated fieldwork and was only engaged in a desk job.

A receptionist called Ragini at her desk.

"Hello Ragini, there is someone in the lobby to meet you."

Ragini was perplexed about who it could be. Since she had left the field job, there were hardly any visitors for her. It was the first time in the last couple of years that someone had come to meet her.

Ajay was sitting in the waiting room. Ragini walked into the lobby and saw someone sitting in the waiting room. She saw it was Ajay. She was shocked. She thought it was better she didn't meet Ajay as she hated him from the core. She knew that Manju's body was stolen by Ajay, but that he was in no way going to admit it.

But Ragini knew that running away from Ajay would not solve anything. So she walked into the room with a smile as if she didn't know him.

Ajay said, "Hello Ragini, how are you?"

"I am good, but sorry I don't recognize you. Have we met before?" Ragini asked as if she was meeting him for the first time.

"No, but you must have heard my name many times. Once you know who I am, you will hate me to the core," Ajay said.

"Who are you?" Ragini asked.

"I am Ajay," Ajay said and got up from the seat.

Ragini remained quiet for a while and said, "There is nothing for you here, Ajay. I lost my sister because of you. You finished everything. What do you want now?"

"It's not what you think, Ragini. I loved your sister as much as you loved her. Or probably more than that," Ajay paused.

"Losing Manju was like losing my purpose to live. There is nothing for me in this world. The only person I want to meet is her daughter. At least, I can see Manju's soul in Hema. I want to meet her before I leave the city forever."

"Hema? I don't know where Hema is," Ragini said in a stern voice.

"Don't hide the truth, Ragini. It's important for me. I know you took her with you after Manju died. And who else will take care of Hema after her mother? It must be you," Ajay looked at Ragini knowingly.

"Even if I knew where she was, I would not let you know. You are a monster Ajay. First you killed my sister, and now you are looking for her daughter," Ragini said in a loud voice.

Ajay remained calm.

"Look, I came here for a purpose. And the purpose is Hema. If you don't want to tell me where she is, then fine. But she won't remain hidden for long. One day I will find her, and then maybe you will never see her again."

Ragini was in shock. She stood there looking at Ajay leaving. The first thing she needed to do was take Hema to a safe place as soon as possible. The best option was to leave the city. After three months, Ragini was to retire. She decided that she would then take Hema away with her.

Ragini would feel alone in the office when Aditi went out for fieldwork. In a brief span of time, Aditi has garnered a lot of positive reactions for her work. She was a star among the other staff. Ragini wanted to find a way to keep Aditi close to her till she retired. Doing this would cure Ragini's loneliness. She did this by telling her Ajay and Manju's story, the one which never happened. The one which was not true.

Ajay kept looking for Hema, but he didn't get any clue. Then one day, he decided to stalk Ragini. Ragini realized that she was being followed by Ajay. To keep Ajay away from Hema, she decided not to meet Hema too frequently. Soon after, Ragini told Aditi about Ajay and Manju. She spoke about Hema too. Aditi was shocked to know that Ragini was Hema's aunt. But Aditi hid the fact from Ragini that she knew Hema. She didn't want to disclose her own dreadful past to Ragini.

On her last day in the office, Ragini decided to leave the city with Hema. After saying her goodbyes, she went directly to the mental hospital to get Hema discharged. But she was shocked to know that Hema had left the hospital a few days back. Ragini thought that once again Ajay had taken Hema away from her. She asked around about who had come to get Hema, but no one had an answer. The recorded name and address was all fake.

Ragini broke down and felt that she had lost everything in her life. There was nothing left in the city for her. So, she decided to leave the city without Hema.

Ajay was still in the city searching for Hema. He was filled with despair. Manju had left him. He hadn't been able to complete his rituals as per Akalkhand, and now, Hema was nowhere to be found. But this time, he was desperate for his hunt. Hunt for Hema's heart. And to complete what Akalkhand said.

9
Doctor Doctor

Ravi reached home and was dead tired. He kept wondering why Ratan had lied to him about the accident. It had never happened that either of them had had to hide anything from the other.

Ravi knew that Ratan was hiding something from him. It was both perplexing as well as hurtful.

On the other side, Aditi reached her house. Her apartment was in the heart of the city.

She parked her car in the basement and went up to the lift. The lift was stuck on the ground floor. It was a very common occurrence as sometimes kids would forget to close the lift door. Aditi didn't have any other option but to take the stairs.

Tired and sleepy, she started to climb the stairs. After a few steps, she felt a sharp pain in her ankles. It felt like someone had pierced a needle in her ankle. The pain was so sharp and torturous that she screamed out loud and sat there holding the ankle with both her hands. The security guard on the ground floor heard her screams and rushed to the basement. He saw Aditi sitting on the stairs holding her foot. He quickly grabbed the first-aid box and ran towards her.

"Do you need some pain relief spray, madam?" he asked.

Aditi nodded, wincing with pain, but her eyes remained closed.

The security guard took out the spray, pointed the nozzle at the ankle and sprayed. It brought her immediate relief. After a few minutes, she relaxed a bit and took a deep breath to calm down. It was evident from her face that the pain had reduced.

"Is it better, madam? Do you need any help to the lift?" the guard asked.

Aditi shook her head and with a wave of her hand said, "No, I will manage."

She got up slowly. She started to walk as if the pain had completely gone.

The guard said, "Shall I get the lift for you, madam?"

Aditi growled loudly and said in a strange voice, "Stay there! I will go myself."

The voice was so terrifying that the security guard dropped the first aid kit from his hand and stood there looking at Aditi climbing up the stairs. He was shocked to hear Aditi's voice change dramatically as if it was someone else speaking to him. Aditi reached her house. She sat on the sofa and then lay down thinking about what had happened yesterday with Dr. Parichit. She started to remember the incident that had happened just before she fainted. She tried to concentrate, but all she could remember was sitting on the chair, switching on the voice memo app and that's it.

She said to herself, "Why can't I remember what happened? Why is it all a blank? What happened to me? Oh god! How do I find out?"

Frustrated, talking to herself, she looked at the iPad. Her eyes stopped at the voice memo app. It struck her that she had switched on the voice memo app just before Dr. Parichit's interview. It meant that the entire interview conversation between her and Dr. Parichit would have been recorded. She quickly clicked on the play button to listen to the recording.

Lying on his bed, Ravi was thinking about Aditi. He tried to remember every word that she had said in the whole day. Every moment spent with her was a gift. He kept thinking about how different Aditi was when they had first met. Right from the lunch date till this night. He scanned through each and every word she had said to him. Ravi was trying to understand the real Aditi.

He knew that she was an independent, ambitious girl with a focused mind. She worked and talked like a boss and could handle difficult situations. She could be a beast when required, but at the same time, she could be all feminine when required. She was soft-hearted, talkative, a person with a golden heart. She was passionate, affectionate, spiritual, and selfless.

"God knows who will be the lucky person with whom she decides to spend all her life. Ah, who will be the lucky one?"

There were some instances where he felt puzzled by the way she had reacted towards him. When Ravi had asked her about depositing the cheque, she had responded very differently. That face he saw in the car park. Her sudden disappearance from the temple, and later when he found her sleeping in the car. Ravi took out his phone and texted her.

"Did you reach safely? Let me know if you need any help. Ratan is doing well. God knows what has happened to him. He met with an accident yesterday night."

He sent the WhatsApp message and kept looking at the phone, waiting for two blue ticks. He kept looking at it for a couple of minutes, but she was not online. Ravi got up and chucked the phone to the other side of the bed. As he was leaving the room, the phone buzzed and he jumped in excitement and grabbed the phone. The message was from Aditi.

"Yes, I have reached. And thanks for asking!"

The phone rang.

He quickly picked up the call and said, "Hey Aditi!"

"What should I say now? At least have a look at your phone to see who is calling you!" Ratan said.

"Ah, you? How are you feeling?" Ravi asked.

"I think you need a doctor more than me." Ratan chuckled.

"Cut that off, Ratan. Tell me what happened?" Ravi asked.

"I need to see the doctor today evening. Mummy is asking me to take you along. So, come home around 5 pm sharp," Ratan said.

"Okay, but when you told the doctor that it was an accident, did he believe your story?" Ravi asked.

"What's there to not believe? Don't you believe it?" Ratan chuckled.

"Ask yourself, Ratan," Ravi paused and continued, "Anyway, I will come down."

Ravi hung up the phone and went downstairs.

That evening, Ravi took Ratan to the hospital. They both went in and waited for the doctor in the lobby.

Ratan saw Ravi looking at his WhatsApp frequently. He asked with curiosity.

"Are you waiting for her message?"

Ravi frowned and looked at Ratan, "Whose message?"

"Who else? Aditi's," Ratan said.

"Nah, it's nothing like that. She needed to see the doctor, so I told her that I could come down if she needed my help," Ravi said.

"Ravi, may I ask you a question?" Ratan asked hesitantly.

"Hey, since when you have you started taking my permission," Ravi chuckled and continued, "Yes, tell me."

"Don't get aggravated, please. But was Aditi really with you all the time?" Ratan asked.

"What has happened to you, Ratan? How many times will you ask me the same question? Yes, she was," Ravi replied.

"I told you, don't get provoked. I am just asking. Keep calm. I mean, seriously, how can any girl tolerate you for so long? I am surprised," Ratan teased.

"Ah-ha, there you go. Jealous, huh?" Ravi countered.

"Yeah, I mean, how come someone like you can get such a beautiful and soft-hearted girl. Lucky!" Ratan said.

"I am not in a relationship, please. But sometimes..." As Ravi was speaking, a nurse came out from the doctor's room.

"Ratan Gandhi!"

Ratan waved his hand and went in with her to the doctor's cabin. While Ravi was sitting there waiting for Ratan, he saw a small boy beside him. The boy waved his hand and smiled. The boy was sitting with his father.

To kill time, Ravi thought of talking to the boy, so he asked, "What happened to you?"

"I don't know. My dad doesn't like me talking to my brother. So, he wants me to see the doctor," the boy replied.

"That's quite strange. Why doesn't he let you talk to him?"

"They say I become a bad boy when I meet him," the boy replied.

Ravi was confused about what he was saying.

"Why do you do that? Where is your brother?" Ravi asked.

The boy pointed his finger at the chair next to him.

Ravi looked at the chair, it was empty. He was baffled.

A nurse came out asking the boy's name. The boy went in along with his father.

An hour later, Ratan came back after dressing his wound.

"All set? Shall we go?" Ravi asked.

"Yeah, I just need to grab some medicine from the store. Let's go there."

They went to the medical store, and Ravi saw the boy's father. Ravi was curious about what exactly had happened to the boy.

"Sorry, but if I may ask, what happened to your kid? Why don't you let him speak to his brother?" Ravi frowned.

"What should I say? He doesn't have any brother. That's it," the father replied and walked out of the store.

Ravi was puzzled and stunned at what he had just heard. At that moment he realized what the kid meant when he pointed his finger at the empty chair. He ran towards the kid's father.

"Sorry, I am confused. What is wrong with your boy?" Ravi asked.

"He has a psychological problem. He sees an imaginary boy around him, and he thinks that boy is his brother. He often plays with him when no one is there in the house. When we ask him about it, he becomes aggressive and sometimes so angry that he throws things at us. One day he threw a knife at me. It is becoming a dangerous situation day by day now. So, we wanted to see the doctor. That's it," his father paused, looked around, and said, "Some people even say that he can see ghosts."

Saying this, the father walked away.

Ratan came to Ravi after taking the medicine from the store and tapped his shoulder.

"What happened?"

Ravi was in deep thought about what that person had said. He looked at Ratan and said,

"That boy," and he kept looking at the kid and his father and said,

"Nothing, nothing. Let's go."

They started to walk towards the scooter, and he received a message from Aditi.

"Hey, if you are free tomorrow morning, do you want to accompany me to the doctor?"

Ravi was blushing now.

Ratan looked at him and said, "Romeo boy! When are you meeting her next?"

"Tomorrow morning," Ravi replied promptly.

"Ratan chuckled and said, "I was thinking of keeping the shop closed for few days. I mean, if you want to open it, then it's fine. Else, there aren't many customers and I can't sit for so long."

"You take rest for few days. I will take care of the shop," Ravi replied.

"Hey, you remember you told me once that someone in your family has this issue of spiritual disease. I mean, someone was possessed, who was that?" Ratan asked with curiosity while walking to the scooter.

"My uncle. My mother's brother. But it has been a couple of years now. Why are you asking?" Ravi asked.

"Nothing, can I talk to them once? Just that this job is creating some interest in me to know more about ghosts and spirits," Ratan replied.

Ravi was watching and listening to Ratan very closely. He felt that since his injury on his head, lately, he was behaving very differently, very mysteriously.

"Okay, let me WhatsApp his number. Just tell him that you're my friend when you speak to him," saying this Ravi shared with Ratan the contact number of his uncle.

"Got it, thanks!" Ratan said.

From the hospital, they both came home.

Ratan thought that the incident with Aditi could be something to do with a spiritual disease. If he wanted to discover what is in the house and who that girl is, he needed to understand how to deal with people who are possessed.

It was evident for Ratan that the girl whose shadow he saw in the blue room was a spirit in the house. Her mother's soul is inside Aditi's body, due to which Aditi had been behaving differently, and the girl thinks that Aditi is her mother. To save Aditi, he needed to free the spirit from the house as well as from Aditi's body. The only person in the world who could help him was someone who treated people possessed with such diseases. Someone like a spirit doctor or a witch doctor.

Thinking about all this, Ratan reached home and dialled Ravi's uncle's number. Initially, it was difficult to strike the conversation with him about what had happened, but somehow, Ratan managed to get the details.

The contact Ratan got was of Sadhu Eknath Maharaj. He got the phone number of one of his disciples, Chhote Maharaj. He managed the time schedule for Sadhu Maharaj, who was busy all the time when not in his *sadhna*.

He dialled Chhote Maharaj.

"Hello, Maharaj ji!"

"Yes, tell me what help do you need?"

"I want to talk to Sadhu Maharaj; can I get an appointment to meet him?"

"Sadhu Maharaj is meditating and will not be talking to anyone for the next couple of days. You can tell me your problem."

Ratan narrated all the incidents that had happened in the house. He also put forward the suspicion about the girl and Aditi being possessed.

"I understand your concern. Please get an answer to one question – how did Aditi come in contact with the house. Did she visit the house before? Because based on your narration, it looks like she is connected somehow to the house and not a stranger to it."

"Sure, Chhote Maharaj. I will find that out and will call you back with all the details."

Chhote Maharaj explained to Ratan that demonic powers need to be verified and cannot take possession without the consent of the host. No matter how minimal it is, there is some connection with the past. There are broadly two ways the power takes control – either by directly passing into the person or with the help of a medium, either witches, wizards or some tantric. Before Chhote Maharaj explained the details to Eknath Maharaj, Ratan needed to provide him Aditi's details.

It was a partial relief for Ratan when he shared what had happened with him, with someone who was an expert in this field. It was ironic that Ratan had started believing in ghosts, which he had never done in his life. Ratan decided that now his work was to investigate Aditi's connection with the house. It would not be as simple as it looked. And the big question still remained, why she had brought Ratan and Ravi into the house, if she really is possessed.

Next morning, Ravi woke up early. His mother was surprised as to what had happened to him. He showered quite early, ate breakfast, and texted Aditi.

"Hey, I am ready. Let me know when you want me to come."

Aditi looked at his message, still in bed. Then she looked at the clock. It was 7 am. Half asleep, she replied to him, "Come by 11. I will WhatsApp you my location."

Aditi was by herself, all alone in her room, and in her life. She had never felt the emptiness of not having anyone around. One of the reasons for that was that she had kept herself so busy in work that she didn't have the time to feel the void around her. It was only at times when she wasn't well, that she felt the loneliness creep in. Especially when all people around you were connected to you in professional capacity. Colleagues will text you a message like "Get well soon" or "Take care of yourself," but what you needed most at such times is someone saying, "You will be fine soon, don't worry, I am there.".

Ravi was slowly filling in that void for Aditi, which Aditi hadn't realized yet. Ravi's number was always on the top of the recently dialled list. He had become the first person she would go to when she needed any help. That morning, Aditi woke up late after replying to Ravi. She freshened up and waited for Ravi to arrive. Till 10:30, she didn't receive any call from him to ask for directions or a flat number, nothing. She looked at her phone twice, thrice just to check if the signal was proper, but it showed full strength. She was getting slightly anxious. This was not the Aditi that used to be. While pacing around the room, she picked up the iPad and looked at the voice memo app. What she heard yesterday was very surprising. She thought of discussing this with Ravi, and suddenly the doorbell rang and startled her.

She said to herself, "Think of the devil, and Ravi is here!" and went forward to open the door.

Ravi was standing there with a smile. He looked at Aditi and said, "Are we ready? Shall we go?"

"I was thinking about you, and you are here. How did you get my apartment number?" Aditi asked.

Ravi smiled and said, "That security guard told me your apartment number."

"Am I that famous?" Aditi chuckled.

Aditi walked out of the flat and closed the door. Then suddenly she opened the door and went in.

Ravi was surprised. Then he saw Aditi coming back with her iPad.

They both went down to the basement.

While they were coming down Ravi asked, "How come you stay alone in the house? Doesn't it get lonely?"

When the door of the elevator opened into the basement, the security guard looked at Aditi, terrified. He started to sweat in no time, as if he had seen something unusually scary. Aditi didn't look at him, but Ravi had seen the guard's reaction.

Ravi, reaching for the car door, asked Aditi, "Did you see that guard? What happened to him? He was shocked when he looked at you!"

"The guard? No, I didn't see that. Why? Not sure what happened to him," Aditi said.

Ravi frowned and sat on the front seat. Aditi was driving the car.

"Ravi, I need to tell you something. Just keep it to yourself. Can you?" Aditi asked.

"Yeah, sure tell me," Ravi replied.

"Don't tell this even to Ratan. I mean, it's a request," Aditi said.

"Why, what happened? Tell me," she said.

"Can you open that voice memo app on my iPad? Just listen to the recording. Can you make out what it says?" Aditi asked.

"Okay," Ravi said and opened the app to listen to the recording.

He heard one lady saying someone something in a strange voice, with a lot of unexplained noise with it. It was as if he was listing to a radio which has captured a very weak signal. There was the sound of someone tapping, the sound of someone laughing crying and growling in between...It was terrifying.

Ravi was still when the recording finished. He looked at Aditi.

"You scared me, Aditi. I can hear some words but faintly. What is that? Whose voice is this?"

"It's my voice!" Aditi said.

Ravi was frozen. He could feel his heart pounding.

"Are you sure? What are you saying?" Ravi frowned.

"Yeah, I had kept this app switched on when I met Dr. Parichit. It recorded the entire conversation between us," Aditi replied.

There was complete silence in the car till they reached the hospital. Aditi stopped the car in the parking.

"Surely, it cannot be me. It must be an issue with the app, the way it got recorded. Do you know how this could happen?" Aditi asked in a small voice.

"I don't know Aditi. It might be that the recording is faulty, or something is wrong with the app."

"Hmm might be," Aditi said.

Then she kept one hand on Ravi's thigh and requested, "Just keep it to yourself. Please!"

Ravi looked at her hand, then into her eyes, and nodded yes.

They both went to the hospital to meet the doctor.

The hospital was one of the biggest in the city. The distance from the parking to the reception was quite a long walk. Ravi was slowly walking behind Aditi. He could smell the perfume Aditi wore; it was sweet with a hint of citrus. They reached the reception. Aditi had an appointment, so the receptionist asked her to sit on the couch in front of the doctor's cabin. Ravi told her that he would go to the washroom and be back. Aditi sat on the couch in front of the doctor's cabin, and Ravi went towards the washroom. After a couple of minutes, when Ravi came out of the washroom, someone tapped him on the shoulder. He turned back and saw a person dressed like a sadhu standing behind him.

Ravi was surprised to see someone like that in the hospital. The sadhu asked,

"Did you come here with that girl?"

Ravi frowned, "Which girl?"

"The reporter. What's her name?" he took a pause and scratched his head

"Yes, Aditi," he replied.

"Why did you bring her here?" the sadhu asked.

"That is none of your business. In fact, this hospital is none of your business. People want to get treated scientifically. I mean, they need a doctor, not people like you," Ravi chuckled.

"You don't know me, boy, that's why you are saying all this. I am Dr. Parichit. I met Aditi during an interview," Dr. Parichit said.

"Oh, I am so sorry," Ravi was surprised to see Dr. Parichit. He could not imagine that Dr. Parichit would look like a sadhu. Submissively, he continued in shallow voice.

"So, you are the one. Nice to meet you sir. I am really sorry. Based on your looks, it's hard to believe that you are the famous Dr. Parichit, Aditi told me about you." Ravi smiled.

"I understand," Dr. Parichit smiled and continued, "Listen, I want to tell you something. You need some other doctor for Aditi."

"Sorry, what do you mean by some other doctor? Do you know any specialist?" Ravi frowned.

"See, Mr..." Dr. Parichit paused.

"Ravi. My name is Ravi," Ravi completed the sentence.

"Yes, Ravi. You need to go to a psychiatric expert," Dr. Parichit answered.

"I am sorry. What do you mean by a psychiatric expert? She is okay, all is well with her," Ravi said.

"This neurosurgeon will not be able to find anything. She needs different care. Different type of doctor," Dr. Parichit replied.

"You mean she needs a psychiatrist or a witch doctor?" Ravi laughed loud.

"Try to understand me, son. I know what she needs," Dr. Parichit insisted.

"See Dr. Parichit. This girl, Aditi is very smart; she knows very well whom to meet and whom not to. Leave that to her. Now leave me alone," saying this Ravi walked to the floor where Aditi was waiting for the doctor. The suggestion that Aditi needed a psychiatrist hurt Ravi.

Dr. Parichit saw Ravi ignoring him and walking towards Aditi. He knew that if this was not stopped now, there was a big disaster waiting in Aditi's life. And it would also impact people who are close to Aditi.

After a while Aditi and Ravi went inside the doctor's cabin.

Aditi explained what was happening to her. She said, "Doctor, I think there is something strange happening to me physically. My vision gets distorted, it's like telescopic vision, or vertigo. It's like when I look at the building in front of me, it either comes together, or falls away, zooms out when I walk on the street. It is very frightening. Sometime I can hear voices, feels like they're coming from inside me. My brain doesn't process things the way it should. It is worrying me doctor, and now I somehow feel things are turning worse."

The doctor listened to her very carefully. After the initial examination he asked Aditi to go for an MRI scan around the brain and neck. While the doctor was talking to Aditi, Ravi asked,

"Doctor, can we spot the problem after the MRI scan? Or do you think these symptoms point towards something else?" Ravi asked, worried.

"Don't worry Ravi. It's a common problem. People suffer from vertigo where they feel dizzy, experience a headache, sweating, nausea, etc. So, let's get the report first, then we will know more," the doctor said keeping that plastic smile on his face.

Aditi got the MRI scan appointment. After coming out from the doctor's cabin, they straight away went to get the MRI.

While Aditi was preparing for MRI, Ravi went to the doctor and asked, "Doctor, do you think that Aditi may need a psychiatrist?" Ravi asked in a worried voice.

"Ravi, you are taking too much stress. It's nothing like that, she will be fine. She doesn't need a psychiatrist. Let's wait for the MRI results," the doctor replied.

"Thanks doctor," Ravi was relieved at the doctor's response. Ravi started to walk out of the doctor's cabin, when a nurse came rushing behind him.

"Sir!"

Ravi looked at her, suspecting that the doctor may have to say something about Aditi. The nurse extended a form and a pen.

"Sir, we need an alternate number other than what madam has given. Please, can you give yours?"

Ravi took the form and wrote his own number on it and gave it back to her.

After the MRI scan was over, Aditi was told that she would be called after a couple of days when the MRI report was ready.

On the other side of the city, Ratan took out his bike and drove it around the lane near his house. He found that he could ride the bike with his head injury, but on the condition that he had to take a lot of small breaks in between for a long-distance ride. He couldn't take a lot of stress. The curiosity to know more about Aditi was killing him. It was no less than a drug that was keeping him high, pushing him to go out and find out more about her.

Around 11 am he left for Aditi's office. He thought of starting from there. He knew Aditi lived alone, so initial information about her could only be obtained from her office colleagues.

Ratan covered the bandage on his head by wrapping a turban like cloth. Since long he had not shaved so anyone who saw him at first glance would say that he was a sardar or Sikh. The name he chose for himself was Jagvir Singh.

After driving for an hour, taking small breaks in between, he reached Aditi's office. He decided that the reason he would use to meet Aditi's colleagues was a story he had and wanted Aditi to write. He knew Aditi wouldn't be there as she was in the hospital with Ravi for the checkup.

Ratan reached the office and went to the reception. He asked the receptionist about Aditi.

"Sure sir, let me dial her extension. Do you have any appointment scheduled with Ms. Aditi?"

Ratan was suddenly nervous. He had thought Aditi was in the hospital, but the receptionist was dialing her number. He stammered and said, "Yes, I had told her that I would be here."

While dialing her extension, the receptionist asked, "Sorry, what's your name sir?"

"I am J…J… Jagvir Singh," Ratan fumbled.

The receptionist dialled the extension and waited. A girl picked up and informed that Aditi was not in the office today.

Ratan was looking around the office, when the receptionist called out, "Mr. Jagvir!"

Ratan didn't look at her. It took him a moment to respond to the name.

"Yes, yes," Ratan answered.

"I am sorry. Miss Aditi is not around. She may have forgotten to tell you that she is on leave today."

"No problem. Please can you ask another staff member to meet me? As I have come from so far, I just want to tell them about me and I will leave after that. Please check with anyone who knows Aditi," Ratan said.

The receptionist dialled a couple of numbers and finally managed to get someone on the call. She looked at Ratan and told him.

"Mr. Jagvir, please wait. Miss Sheetal will attend to you soon. Please wait in the meeting room."

"Thank you very much," Ratan said and sat in the meeting room.

After some time, a girl walked into the room and met Ratan. He narrated the story about him being a farmer in a village near Punjab and his issue with the bank harassing him for loan installments for a tractor he had bought.

Ratan had managed to get Sheetal's attention.

After completing his story, Ratan told Sheetal, "It would have been better if I could have met Aditi."

"Yeah, I know. But sorry, she is on leave today. Don't worry, you give me all your documents. I will tell her about you," Sheetal assured him.

"I don't have any documents with me. But you can narrate my story to Aditi. If you want, I can come back and speak to her again," Ratan replied.

"Okay," the girl paused for few seconds, waited and said, "See you then."

Ratan stood up and said, "May I ask you something?"

"Yeah, sure, "Sheetal replied.

"Is Aditi a talkative person like you?" Ratan smiled and continued, "I mean, does she speak freely?"

"Why are you asking this? I thought you have spoken to her before."

"Yeah, but it was a very brief conversation. So, I am nervous."

"You will be fine. She will listen to you." Sheetal smiled.

"Sorry, but I have heard that she only talks to very few people," Ratan said.

"Look, Mr. Jagvir Singh, you will be fine. Don't worry," Sheetal replied.

"Miss Sheetal, I am just a little cautious. Whom does she speak with most in the office?"

"She used to talk with her mentor a lot. She was her best friend, but now she has left. I mean, she has retired and left the city," Sheetal replied.

"I am sorry Miss. But please, can you tell me her name?" Ratan insisted.

"Looks like you are more interested in Aditi's details. Why are you inquiring so much?" Sheetal asked, suspicious.

"I am really sorry if I have made you feel uncomfortable. I just asked so that it would help to break the ice with Miss Aditi when I speak to her," Ratan said meekly and started to walk out of the room.

While he was walking out, Sheetal said in a loud voice.

"Mr. Jagvir, her name is Ragini Iyer. She stays somewhere in Model Colony. I heard recently from someone that she is back in town. But she didn't meet Aditi when she left the office."

Ratan repeated the name and address in his mind, "Ragini Iyer, Model Colony."

Model Colony was a big locality. Finding someone in that huge area was like finding a needle in the haystack. He reached his bike in the parking lot, when it struck him that he could get Ragini Iyer's contact information from the reception.

He went back to reception, but the only information he could get from her was a phone number. Ratan went down and dialled that number. No one picked up. Ratan decided that he would keep on dialing that number the whole day till someone picked it up.

After a lot of unsuccessful attempts, he decided to speak to the telephone exchange and get the location where the phone was installed. After a long struggle, he finally got Ragini's address. Ratan had hooked his hopes on what Ragini would say about Aditi. He was sure that he would find something about Aditi through Ragini.

The very next day, Ratan went to Ragini's house. The building was two-storied, and she stayed on the ground floor. Model colony was famous for its well-planned area. The houses lined up in neat rows. They all had the same design, the lawns were of the same size, and the houses were sequenced and grouped by alphanumeric. Ragini's house was not that difficult to find due to such a systematic layout and numbering. When Ratan reached the house, there was dead silence. The house had a small lawn, and a pathway which led to the main door. At the entrance of the lawn was an iron gate, which was closed with a simple latch, unlocked. He opened the small gate which made a creaking sound, as if it had not been oiled since long. Crossing the small pathway, he reached the door and rang the bell. There was no response. He pressed the bell a couple of times, but there was no response. There was no lock at the front door that indicated that someone was inside the house. He knocked on the door many times, but there was no response. He peeped through the window; it was dark except for the light coming from one room. He went around the house, peeping through all the windows which were open. While he was scanning each corner of the house, suddenly his eyes noticed someone lying down on the floor. It was apparent that someone had fallen down. Ratan decided to break the door and go in with all his strength. He started to push the main door. But no luck. While slamming the door, he felt a latch on the top of the door, which was holding the door. Just above the door, there was a ventilation gap, covered with one angular piece of glass. He took a long stick, climbed up and tried to open the latch with the stick. After a long struggle, the latch unlocked and the door opened.

Ratan rushed into the room and found an old lady lying unconscious. She was still breathing. Ratan quickly went into the kitchen and brought a glass of water. He sprinkled the water on her face. She opened her eyes. Ratan managed to make her sit on the sofa. She looked confused, and then looking at Ratan in the house, she got afraid.

She shouted, "No, no, don't kill me. I don't know where she is!"

Ratan was baffled at her reaction. He said,

"Madam, I am Aditi's friend. The girl who used to work in your office. You were her mentor. Listen to me please."

It took a while for Ratan to explain that he came to meet her and that he knew Aditi.

Ratan asked her, "Madam, are you okay? Do you need a doctor?"

"Why do you want to know about Aditi?" she asked.

"Madam, I came here looking for you. My name is Jagvir, Jagvir Singh. I am Aditi's friend. And I need some help," he replied.

Ragini calmed down.

"Please get me my tablets, they're there on the shelf," Ragini pointed her finger towards the cupboard.

Ratan went in and scrambled in the medicine box to find the tablet. While he was taking out the medicine, he saw a picture of the two women. Ratan picked up the frame and closely studied it. He could recognize Ragini. The woman next to her looked familiar, but he couldn't place her. He gave her the tablets. She popped one pill and lay down on the sofa, closing her eyes.

Ratan sat there on the chair and waited for her to speak.

10
Shhh...erlock Holmes

Same day morning at Ragini’s house.

Ajay was losing all hope of finding Hema. That day when he went to the doctor’s place, he saw Ragini in the grocery store nearby. He thought that Ragini might be living with Hema. Next afternoon, he broke into Ragini’s house.

“Hello Ragini, nice to see you back in town,” Ajay said, smiling.

Ragini, who had not been keeping well lately, spooked out looking at Ajay. She didn’t say a word as she was in shock.

“See Ragini, I have searched for Hema everywhere, but have not been able to find her. Lucky now that I saw you at the grocery store yesterday. Now tell me where is Hema?” Ajay yelled at Ragini.

“I don’t know where she is. I thought you have taken her away,” Ragini was surprised.

“Me? Do you think this is a joke? See I am tired now, and frustrated too. I am giving you a last chance to spell out where is Hema,” Ajay shouted again.

“She is not with me. For god’s sake, leave us alone. What do you need from us?” Ragini shouted back.

“Heart, I need Hema’s heart. Kaal says, if I get her heart, then I can get my Manju back. I beg you Ragini, tell me where Hema is,” Ajay was on his knees, pleading with folded hands.

“You want to kill Hema?” Ragini stammered, terrified.

Ajay laughed like a maniac and said, "It's a sacrifice for Kaal, Ragini. See, he is watching you and me. He needs Hema's heart to bring Manju back. Anyway, Hema can't live a normal life. Let her at least bring back Manju and let Manju lead a normal life," Ajay kept laughing as he said this. His face was red, his eyes bloodshot, and that laugh sent chills down Ragini's spine.

Finally Ragini said, "I would rather die than tell you where Hema is. You maniac, you crazy bastard!"

In anger, Ajay hit Ragini on her neck and she fainted. Ajay sat near her and said,

"You and your sister. Why are you so adamant? I asked Manju to come with me and had she listened to me, she would have been alive. And you would not be in this condition. What a shame! I will find Hema anyway Ragini, I will find her."

Ravi was in the hospital, and he thought that he would not tell Aditi about his meeting with Dr. Parichit. It would unnecessarily stress her. She was already worked up about that interview and recording on the voice app.

While Aditi and Ravi were coming out of the hospital, Ravi saw Dr. Parichit walking towards the parking lot. One thing that kept bothering him was why an expert like Dr. Parhchit would tell Ravi to show Aditi to a psychiatrist. What had he seen that day? And that voice on the recording. Dr. Parichit must surely remember what had happened that day.

He told Aditi, "Hey, I forgot something in the hospital. You get in the car, I will be back in a moment."

Aditi smiled, "Come soon, I am starving."

Ravi nodded and rushed to the elevator. He reached the parking and saw Dr. Parichit getting into his car.

Ravi ran to the front of the car. Dr. Parichit applied a hard brake. The car screeched to a halt. Dr. Parhchit came out of the vehicle.

"What happened? Is all well?" he asked, worried.

"Yeah, all is well. The doctor has studied Aditi's reports and said that it's a normal symptom of vertigo. He will wait till the MRI report is out," Ravi replied.

Dr. Parichit shook his head in dismay and said, "Your choice, you wait and see the results."

He paused and continued, "But why have you come here?"

Ravi replied, "Dr. Parichit, I know you are a well-known expert in parapsychology. When you spoke to me about Aditi, I should not have taken it lightly. But still, I am sure she doesn't need a psychiatrist. I am just wondering why you said she needed one. And what happened on the day of the interview?"

"Ravi, I witnessed Aditi's behaviour when we met for that interview. The signs I saw that day, it's not normal. I am not saying you need some witch doctor or a tantric, but yes, she needs special care. Now I can see you are with her. Try to stay close to her as much as possible," Dr. Parichit said and walked towards the car. He turned and said, "One more thing. Don't tell her that you met me. She might get disturbed."

Dr. Parichit put one hand in his left pocket, took out his visiting card, and handed it over to Ravi.

"Here is my card! If you feel the need, please speak to me."

Dr. Parichit smiled and walked back to his car.

Ravi stood there watching him go and later came back to Aditi.

He kept looking at her. Aditi looked absolutely normal, there was no sign that indicated that there was something unusual with her.

"Do you want me to drive?" Ravi asked.

"Sure." Aditi smiled.

Ravi sat in the driver seat and asked, "Tell me, where do you want to go? Home or Lash?"

"Good question, dear chauffer," Aditi chuckled and continued, "Lash it is!"

Ravi shook his head, smiled and repeated, "Lash it is!"

Funnily enough, they had all come to call Kailash restaurant Lash, as in a dead body. Only because the board in front of the eatery was broken and the only legible letters were LASH.

They reached Kailash restaurant after a few minutes. He found a spot and they sat down and ordered some snacks and tea.

Ravi felt that Aditi was too quiet.

"Are you feeling fine? Don't worry about the MRI report. Everything will be okay," Ravi said.

Aditi looked at him, smiled, and said, "I know Ravi. But I can't understand what's happening to me nowadays. I don't feel that I am alone. It is like I think I am with someone, always. But what or who it is, I don't know. This is such a perplexing situation that I can't say what exactly it is," Aditi paused.

"Is it because I am stressed? What is that phantom feeling?"

Aditi was quiet, and Ravi knew that he had to say something.

"Why don't you take a break?" Ravi asked Aditi in a low voice.

"Break? What break?" Aditi asked in surprise.

"I mean, you should take a break from work and go out of town. Take a break for a couple of days," Ravi said.

"You might be right, Ravi. But with whom?" Aditi asked and chuckled.

Ravi was almost ready to take his own name, but held back. It was quiet again. The waiter came back with the food, which broke the silence between them.

Ratan was sitting beside Ragini. Waiting for her to wake up, he could see that she was tired and exhausted, but only god knew why that had happened to her. He decided to let her wake up by herself. After an hour and a half, Ragini woke up and looked at Ratan.

Ratan asked, “How are you feeling now? What happened to you? I saw you lying down on the floor.”

Ragini sat on the sofa, leaned backwards completely and Ajay’s face flashed in her mind.

She said, “Someone came here to find something, unfortunately I didn’t have what he was looking for. So, he returned the favor by hitting me on my neck. I fainted.” She took a pause and asked, “Leave that, what is your name? Why did you come here?”

“Oh gosh, should we call the police?” Ratan said.

“No, it’s fine. Police won’t be of any help. You tell me who you are and why you are here.”

“I am Jagvir Singh. I want to know something about Aditi. Would you help me?” Ratan asked.

“Who?” Ragini frowned.

“You worked with her in the press before. You were her mentor,” Ratan asked Ragini, expecting that she would remember.

“Oh, Aditi. Yeah, I know her,” Ragini replied to him with a depressed face.

“I thought you were close to her.,” Ratan said curiously.

Ragini smiled and replied, “If god gives me an option to unmeet someone in my life, she would be the second one. After my sister.”

Ratan did not expect that response. It was exactly the opposite of what he had thought. He looked at her and said, "I am sorry to hear that. But I was under the impression that you guys got along very well."

"She often used to take suggestions from me about work. I never shied away from telling her that. But…" and Ragini stopped.

Ratan waited for few seconds for her to respond, but she didn't say a word.

"But what Ragini? I want to know," Ratan asked.

"Jagvir, why are you here?" Ragini said and continued, "I am done with all relationships in my life; they are all dead connections for me – friends, family, everyone. Please excuse me."

"I am sorry, Ragini. I can understand how it feels. I am sorry for that. And I promise that I am not here to hurt you in any way. I just want some answers, then I will leave. That's it," Ratan said.

"What do you want to know? Tell me," Ragini questioned.

"How about we talk it over a cup of tea? I will make it for you," Ratan smiled and asked. He knew before striking any conversation with Ragini about Aditi it was critical to make her comfortable.

Ragini smiled and said, "Okay, the kitchen is that side," she pointed towards the other room.

While making tea, Ratan spoke to her about general things to get her to relax.

After a few minutes, tea was ready, and they both sat at the dining table. Ragini's house was well arranged. She had very few things in the house. She was the perfect example of a person following a minimalist lifestyle.

The house had a sense of calmness.

"Now you tell me what you want to know?" Ragini asked Ratan. She was looking better, but her neck still hurt.

"Who is Aditi? Anything you want to share," Ratan asked.

"Aditi is a nice girl. Good at her job. Always on-time, dedicated, hardworking, and focused. She did not indulge in gossip or mingle much with people, but was always ready to help if anyone asked her," Ragini said.

"Did you see or experience anything unusual when you were with her? Anything at all?" Ratan asked.

"What exactly do you mean? She was a normal girl," Ragini insisted.

"Just think, did you at any point feel that she is not Aditi, but someone else?" Ratan asked.

"Who are you, Jagvir? How are you connected to Aditi? Tell me!" Ragini asked with suspicion.

"I am her friend," Ratan asked.

"No, Jagvir. Tell me, who are you? Why are you here? Aditi has no friends. I know that," Ragini asserted.

Ratan knew that if he wanted information from Ragini, he had to tell her something which would convince her. He was afraid that if he revealed everything about that house or Aditi, it might jeopardize his meeting with Ragini. He decided to make up a story that was close to the truth, but not exactly true.

"Ragini, I had to meet Aditi professionally for one assignment. I submitted my write-up to her. That day when I met her in the office meeting room for work, I found her behaviour very strange. The way she spoke and reacted…it was not Aditi, but someone else. I was terrified and agreed to whatever she wanted me to edit. I have seen people in my village behaving strangely, as if some supernatural power is guiding them. They were possessed by demons. I found Aditi behaving in a similar way. If there is any way in which I can help her, I would like to. I tired speaking to people in the office, but no one knows Aditi very well other than you. So, I thought of meeting you to know more about her," Ratan replied and looked at Ragini.

Ratan was praying that Ragini would be convinced with his story.

"I have never seen Aditi the way you are describing her. She was always normal. I think I have shared what I had to. I have nothing more for you," Ragini got up and went to keep her teacup in the kitchen.

"Then why did you say that she is someone you want to unmeet in your life? What are you hiding from me Ragini? If you think Aditi needs some help, then we should help her," Ratan said.

Ragini stood near the kitchen platform, looking at the teacup. Ratan continued, "If you don't want to help, I will not ask you to. At least, let me help her. And for that, I need to know more about Aditi. Is there something you want to share? I beg you, please!" Ratan said and waited for Ragini to respond.

"I don't believe in demonic possession, but Aditi defies my belief."

Ragini replied in a toneless voice.

Ratan was not shocked.

"Do you think she is possessed? Why do you say so?" Ratan asked.

"I have seen her change and speak like someone I know, who is dead now. Surprisingly, none other than my sister," Ragini said, her voice breaking

"Your sister?" Ratan stammered.

"Manju," Ragini said and started to weep slowly.

"This is the reason I told you, Jagvir, don't bring those memories back. They haunt me day and night. I have tried hard to come out of it, but it feels like in this lifetime, I will not be able to come out of it," Ragini sat on the chair, holding her face.

Ratan was shocked to hear Manju's name. He swiftly ran back to the cupboard where the medicine was kept and took out the picture from there. He took out the photo and kept it in his wallet, the picture that was taken from the house. He was stunned to see that they both matched. Ragini was Manju's sister.

Things were getting more and more tangled up for Ratan. He had come to meet Ragini to know about Aditi, but there was much more to the story.

He kept the photo back in the wallet. He showed Ragini the picture he had taken out from the cupboard and asked her, "Is this your sister, Manju?"

Ragini looked at the picture and said, "Yes."

Ratan said, "If you don't mind, can you tell me more about Aditi and what could have triggered Manju to stay in Aditi."

"It's all my fault. I should not have told Aditi about her," Ragini said.

Ratan asked, "Please can you tell me more? What exactly happened? I need to know everything from the beginning."

Ragini began, "When I first meet Aditi in the office, she was a simple, innocent and submissive girl. I was about to retire in a year, so the boss decided that it would be good for me to mentor Aditi. He didn't want me to get loaded with work. His father had hired me for the job, and he had a lot of respect for me."

Ragini stood up, brought the water bottle, poured some water in the glass, and gulped. She continued, "Aditi had the drive to learn, so much so, that she never wanted to go out with her colleagues. I asked her to make some friends in town, but she always dodged my suggestions. When she had joined work, she didn't have a place to stay. I deliberately found one place in the heart of the city. At least she could go out at night after work, if she felt like it. The lighting on the streets and the lively market might entice her to move around the city and she might make some friends in the café or in the market. But that never happened. She was a loner, and she never regretted being one. I didn't know from where she came or who her parents were. She always said that it was all in her past, and she wanted to come out of it. It must be a painful past. She didn't want to remember her past life and ruin the happiness of her present. She never told me much about her past," Ragini smiled and gulped down another glass of water.

Ratan asked, "Then what happened after that? What changed?"

Ragini said, "Aditi was a stranger to me. I only knew what she was in the office. After some point, I didn't have much to talk to Aditi, and she also kept herself busy. Slowly we became close and she became like a daughter to me. So, I missed talking to her when she was not around. Once, I told her about my sister Manju. I told her how our childhood was and how we grew up. She started to take interest in that story. Whenever I used to talk about Manju, she would be most interested. Manju was similar to Aditi. She was also a loner, no friends, she knew only me. She was also hard-working and a bookworm."

Ragini continued, "One day I told Aditi that Manju had stayed in the same city after marriage. She wanted to see that house. Not a single day passed when Aditi didn't come to me and asked me if we would go to see that house. I am not sure why she wanted to go to the place. I never got the answer from her. Whenever I asked her, she replied that she wanted to see Manju's place where she lived. I always laughed at that. But at that time, I didn't know I was inviting serious trouble for her and making the most horrible mistake of my life," saying this, Ragini took a deep breath.

Ragini continued, "Manju was a marvelous doctor and the best surgeon a hospital could get. She kept herself busy in her job and lately she had started coming home late. One day I found a book related to occult practices. I thought that she might be reading it to take a break from her busy schedule. Then one day, I heard a phone conversation between her and another doctor. They talked about taking a piece of cloth soaked in the blood of the patient and meeting at the cremation ground. I was terrified when I heard the way Manju was talking about it. She was never like that."

Ratan cut her in between and asked, "Who was that doctor she was talking to? Did you find out his name?"

Ragini replied, "I tried asking Manju many times about it, but she never told me. When I inquired secretly around the hospital, people said she met a lot with a junior doctor named Ajay."

That name was like a thunderbolt for Ratan.

"Manju was one day caught by her senior consultant when she was taking that blood soaked cloth. People in the hospital knew about it, and there was a rumour that she would indulge in these practices. But it was also a fact that she was a fantastic surgeon. So, the senior doctor wanted her to stay in the hospital. One day when she came back home, I had a big argument with her about it. When I confronted her, she said that she was saving the life of a small girl by burning one of her organs in the cremation ground under the guidance of some aghori. I wanted to go to the police about it. But it was my love for her that I never did. My relationship with her as a sister was not the same after that incident. One day I heard she was to marry one of the richest guys in town. I thought at least after marriage, she will be a changed woman, but I was wrong. Manju was so much involved in it that she did the same practice on her daughter. And the result was that her daughter suffered severe psychological trauma and she had to be put into a mental hospital. Her marriage went through serious trouble. Her husband stayed at home most of the time. The business went into loss, and he lost almost everything. Manju was now not that Manju, but she was transformed into something like a witch doctor. One day I heard the news that Manju and Ram's bodies were found in the house. No one knew what happened exactly. When the doctor conducted the postmortem, they didn't find anything there. Their death is a mystery till date. After the postmortem, I went to the hospital to collect her body to complete the final rituals. To my shock, when I reached there, I heard that her body had been stolen from the mortuary. I filed a police complaint. There was an investigation, but the body was never found. I am sure Ajay had done this."

Ragini started to weep, keeping her head down on the table.

Ratan asked, "Did you tell all this to Aditi?"

Ragini was weeping and shook her head in disagreement. She continued her story with tears in her eyes, "How can I tell this to Aditi? How can a girl tell such a story about her sister? Manju was my everything after our parents left. So, I changed the narration and built a beautiful love story between Manju, Ajay and Ramchandani. I made Manju the person who sacrificed everything in her life. What else could I have done? And while I was narrating the story to Aditi, she was taking more and more interest in her life. To ensure that Aditi stayed around me more in the office, I made Manju the ideal woman. But that story changed Aditi's life. One day after a lot of insisting, I went to the house with her. I showed the house to her from afar. I never wanted to go inside the house. So, I made up some stories about spirits in Manju and Ramchandani's house and warned her that she should not go inside."

Ratan asked Ragini in wobbling voice, "What triggered Manju to get involved in occult practices? It's hard to believe that someone with such brilliance would ever be involved in it."

Ragini replied, "After Manju's death, I tried to get the answers from the people in the hospital. But no one knew how it had started. Everyone mentioned a patient with whom Manju was involved. Nurses say that it was because of him that Manju began to read stories around these practices."

Ratan was speechless. He never thought that he would get to know a bitter truth about Manju. But, the mystery was yet unsolved. Ratan asked, "When did you know that Manju had possessed Aditi?"

Ragini took a sip of water and continued, "I didn't know what exactly happened, but one day I went with Aditi to her house. She had invited me for dinner. It is not usual for her to invite someone for dinner. I might have gone once or twice before. But that day, she insisted that I come for dinner to her house. After dinner, we were, as usual, talking about Manju. I said that Manju's ghost was around the house and she should stay away from there. After a minute, Aditi's voice changed. She started to talk to me like Manju. I still remember that face; her eyes rolled up, she slowly sat on the sofa in a squatting position, with both her hands on her back. Her sinister, demonic voice with growling in between. I was so terrified that I nearly fainted. She kept saying that same line, 'How much will you lie about your sister?' This is the line she repeated; growling, smiling, and screaming in between. To my surprise, the story which I had made up about the house being inhabited with spirits of Manju and Ramchandani, was in fact true. I shouted at Aditi and asked her if she had gone in the house.

Manju's voice answered, "Yes, and she now knows everything."

After a few minutes Aditi fell asleep and I left.

Ragini stopped and looked outside. It was almost midnight. Ratan was worried after listening to that story. What he had just heard was something he could never have thought by any stretch of the imagination.

"Did you meet Aditi after that day?" Ratan asked Ragini.

"Yes, I did meet her. But she was normal. As if nothing had happened. I also didn't tell her anything about Manju. That was my last month in the office."

Ragini took a deep breath and said again, "If god gives me a chance, I will unmeet these people in my life. I regret being Manju's sister and Aditi's mentor."

Ratan was confused. He had nothing to ask or say. Both he and Ragini sat quietly. Ragini felt a sense of calm after she had told that story to Jagvir. At least someone else too knew the truth now. It was as if she had thrown off the burden that she had been carrying for so long.

After few minutes, Ratan said, "I don't have anything to say Ragini. What you have told me, it's terrible and I feel very sorry for you. You have been a fantastic sister and mentor. Now, please take care of yourself. Your phone is not working, please make sure it does. I will keep coming to your house, just to see if all is okay with you. Thanks a lot." Ratan stood up. "It is quite late. I must go. And I have a request to make. If Aditi asks you about me, please don't say anything. This is the only way I can help her, by doing my work silently," Ratan said and walked out of the house.

That night, Ratan didn't sleep. What Ragini had said was exactly the opposite of what Aditi had told Ratan and Ravi. The difference was that Ragini had told about her sister's past and Aditi had recounted what she had heard from Ragini. There was no reason to doubt Ragini's story. The next task at hand was to find a way to make sure that Ravi was safe with Aditi and to free Aditi from Manju's possession. That reminded him about Chhote Maharaj. Ratan had enough background on what exactly had happened with Aditi.

Ravi was coming back to his house on his scooter after dropping Aditi to her home. In the lane near his house, he saw a man holding the same helmet Ravi had punched a few days back. The helmet had a white patch. The man was walking with his head tilted to one side. Ravi thought that it might be because he had hit him very hard that day. Ravi felt sad. He thought of asking him how he was feeling and also apologize. But as soon as Ajay saw Ravi coming towards him, he sat on his bike and took off from there. Ravi had seen his face; he was in his late 50s or early 60s. This troubled Ravi more than anything else, that he had actually hit an elderly man.

When he reached home, Ravi tried his best to convince himself that Aditi didn't need any psychiatrists. On the other hand, how could Dr. Parichit, who was so confident, be wrong in assessing Aditi? But, how can you bring someone you love, to see a psychiatrist? *I know Aditi is fit and fine; she is a normal girl, no, I mean she a special girl. Even though my love might be like a one-way street, but I am on it. And this highway has no exit route.*

Dr. Parichit had told Ravi about Aditi's behaviour. Ravi too had witnessed a few instances where Aditi was behaving differently. There was something not quite right with her.

Ravi decided that he would ask Ratan to go with him into the house to explore more. Was there something inside in the house which had an impact on Aditi and the way she had been behaving recently? There were two immediate problems in front of Ravi. Firstly, Ratan was not in a condition to move around, and the second was that Ratan didn't like that Ravi was so deeply involved with Aditi.

The only option for Ravi was to go into the house alone and see if he could find something that would point to any paranormal activity.

The next day, Ravi decided to go into the house in the morning instead of at night. He reached the house around 10 am. It was bright daylight, and the light was enough to penetrate through the windows in the house. He parked his scooter on the lawn and stood there. He looked at the house from there. As usual, there was no noise of any sort except of the leaves rattling and birds chirping. Someone tapped him on his shoulder.

He shouted, "Who is this?" and ran towards the scooter.

He was the same guy who used to sit outside the house. He smelled like rotten meat, as if he had never showered and had covered himself with a black blanket. He had long nails and laughed like a maniac, "Do you have food?"

Ravi shouted, "You idiot. Get the hell out of here. You almost killed me!" and chased him out. The house looked the same as on day one, when they both had come with Aditi. It looked gloomy, with broken windows, curtains on the top floor blowing in the wind. Ravi said a silent prayer, kissed his locket with lord Shiva's picture, touched the thread around his arm, and touched the ground. He felt like he was going to a warzone. To take that first step, it took him around five minutes. Ravi started to keep one foot in front of another slowly, with shaky legs. While walking towards the door, he kept humming lord Shiva's name.

He reached the door and held the doorknob. He waited there and peeped through the window to see inside. It was quiet. He was glancing across the hall to see inside, when suddenly, a face appeared in front of him in a flash and stood there. It was a jolt for Ravi to see that. She was looking at him eye to eye. Ravi was cold, his heart was pounding, and his forehead was covered with sweat. The girl gave a ghostly smile but in a few seconds, that terrifying face burst into laughter. Ravi started to cry.

"Don't kill me. Don't kill me, please!"

The girl, while laughing, suddenly vanished. He was now sure that she was the ghost in the house. He thought that the same spirit must have possessed Aditi. In that moment, a hand appeared on the window pane as if someone was getting up from the floor holding the window frame. That hand had blood stains on it. Ravi thought that the girl would crawl out of the window and grab him, so he stepped back.

The girl stood up again and looked at Ravi. With the dark circles, white complexion and light blue patches on her face, she looked terrifying. She slowly rose as though she was floating in the air. Ravi's complete body was numb, he couldn't even feel the gravel hurting his back. She again disappeared in the blink of an eye. Ravi was sure he had seen a ghost in the house. Even though Ravi was terrified of that face, his love for Aditi was much stronger. He had two options in front of him – either go back home or go inside and find out who the ghost was so that he could talk to her and free Aditi.

He stood up, chanting lord Shiva's name and went near the window. There he screamed.

"Who is inside the house? Are you the one who has possessed Aditi? Leave her alone, okay?"

He opened the door and went inside the house. Love can do wonders, and Ravi was a living example of it. There was pin drop silence. There was no sign of the girl who had appeared on the window.

While he was standing in the main hall on the ground floor, he heard some footsteps on the top floor. The shutters of windows rattled loudly. He could hear a girl giggling out loud.

He went near the curved staircase and started to climb the stairs slowly. He was climbing up one step at a time quietly, so as not to make any sound. The sound of the girl giggling continued. Every step he took to climb upstairs elevated his heartbeat also. The only name he took the whole time was of lord Shiva to keep him calm. But it did not work. Those stairs must have been the toughest climb for Ravi in his life. Finally, he reached the passage with the two rooms on each side. That giggling never stopped, and it was coming from one room. It was the same room with the blue decor.

He shouted, "Who is there?"

The giggling stopped.

Ravi called out meekly now, "See whoever is there, please tell me who you are. I am here to make a request to you. I need your help. Please don't play games with me."

There was complete silence. Then suddenly, the giggling started, followed by hiccups. A girl came crawling on her fours. She was wearing a white dress. She came out and sat near the door, looking at Ravi.

Ravi looked at her and started chanting lord Shiva's name louder. The girl, when she saw that, burst into laughter which was intermittently interrupted by hiccups. At that moment, the only thing he relied upon was the locket of Shiva and the thread around his arm.

Ravi looked at her. That terrifying face had a hint of beauty. For a few seconds, he felt that the laughter was not of a ghost but of an innocent teenage girl. Then in a moment, he realized that it could be because the ghost was hypnotizing him. It might be a trap.

Ravi folded his hands and pleaded.

"Please leave me alone. I came here for Aditi. Please stay away from her."

The girl looked at Ravi and then became quiet. She turned back to go inside the room. While she was turning back, a nail jutting out of the door frame scratched her arm. She screamed, and swiftly ran inside the room.

Ravi saw that the nail had peeled the skin from her arm. It stunned him, and he said to himself, "How can a nail hurt a ghost? Don't they have the power to go through walls?"

Now Ravi thought that she might not be a ghost, but pretending to be one. Ravi followed her. He was shocked to see that there was no one there. It was empty.

This gave him the chills and he was confused again. How could she disappear from the room? She had just crawled inside the room a few minutes back. His heartbeat spiked. He swiftly rushed towards the window, thinking that she might have jumped from there. When he looked outside, he realized that no one could jump from that height and survive. That room suddenly became a bigger mystery. While he was thinking all this, he looked at the floor. It had tiny drops of blood going to the small cupboard which was stuck to the wall. He bent and touched one of the drops; it was wet. He guessed that it was the girl's blood when she got a scratch from the nail. He slowly walked towards the cupboard and quickly pulled open the door. It was empty. Looking at the blood drop and the way she had screamed because of the nail, Ravi was partially convinced that she was not a ghost but a human. A live and breathing girl.

Back in Ratan's house, Ratan had called up Chhote Maharaj, and narrated in detail the story he had heard from Ragini about Aditi and Manju. Maharaj listened to Ratan carefully, without saying a word. After Ratan had finished the story, Chhote Maharaj told him.

"See Ratan, from what you have told me, it looks like she is possessed and the spirit is aggressive. Manju was doing occult practices when she was alive, it means she will be more powerful now, after her death. Until I discuss this with Sadhu Eknath Maharaj and find a solution, I ask you to remain vigilant. Please don't go near her. But if by any chance you come face to face with her, chant this mantra '*Om Sham Shanicharaya Namaha*'. Don't speak anything else while chanting. If she provokes you to talk, don't ever use the words ghost, spirits, demon, black magic, etc. Don't let her know or make her feel by your behavior that you have seen her in *preta avataram*. Behave as if you was are unaware that she is possessed by Manju. Most importantly, it may be dangerous for people who are close to her. So keep yourself and your loved ones away from her as much as you can."

When Ratan heard that he should keep his dear ones safe from Aditi, Ravi's face flashed in front of him. Chhote Maharaj continued, "And do not worry. We will find a solution after I speak to Sadhu Eknath Maharaj."

11
Bunker

It was not like Ratan to believe in ghosts or spirits. He had always believed in living a spiritual life. For him, it was hard to believe that a person could transform herself into another person and become so powerful that she could pick up that table with one hand, and swing it towards him like a frisbee.

Ratan looked at the table kept beside his bed where all of his medicines were kept. The table was roughly about the same size as the one Aditi had picked up. He removed all the medicines and tried to pick it up with one hand. He did manage to pick it up, but it was too heavy to be swung. He kept it down, and it confirmed that Aditi couldn't pick it up. It would have to be some external force that had helped her do that.

That evening he had an appointment for the dressing of his stitches. Ratan decided that he would go alone to get some time to think and how best he should ask Ravi to move away from Aditi without divulging the details. He picked up his bike and drove towards the hospital. While riding the bike, he thought about Manju, Gangaram hospital, and thought that he could get some clues about Manju and the occult practices she was involved with. He reached the hospital and waited for his turn in the lobby. A nurse called him up for dressing the stitches. He walked into the room, busy in all those thoughts of Gangaram Hospital, muttering under his breath. The nurse heard him and while cleaning the stitches, asked him.

"What happened in Gangaram Hospital?"

"I am looking for someone who would know a surgeon who worked long ago in that hospital. Someone named Dr. Manju," Ratan replied.

"My mother used to work in Gangaram Hospital. She retired from there," the nurse smiled.

"Will she know Dr. Manju? She was a surgeon in the 80s," Ratan frowned and looked at her.

"I can ask. Do you want me to call her now?" The nurse stopped for a brief second and looked at Ratan.

"That would be a great help," Ratan replied, trying to curb his excitement.

"Okay, let me finish with this dressing first, and then I will call her," she said.

After a few minutes, she finished the dressing and sat beside a table near Ratan. Ratan found her sitting close, very close. In her late twenties, she was slightly plump with a height of around 5 feet 5-inches, clear skin tone, with glossy skin. Ratan did not mind the room filled with an antiseptic and unpleasant smell anymore. She wore a subtle rose perfume, which could only be smelled if someone sat in close proximity. In a moment, Ratan felt a soothing sense of calm that he had not felt lately.

The nurse finished that call with her mother. He tried to look at the nurse's badge, but he couldn't see the name. It was turned downwards. The nurse saw Ratan trying hard to know her name so she said,

"Kavya!" she looked at Ratan with the poker face.

Ratan replied with a smile, "Thanks Kavya, what did your mother say?"

"She didn't know anyone with that name in Gangaram Hospital," Kavya replied.

Ratan was surprised to hear that. Dr. Manju was such a famous name in that hospital. He thought for a while and said, "Oh! Thanks Kavya. We took a chance, but hard luck."

After the dressing was finished, Ratan started to walk out, and said, "May I say something Kavya?"

"Yes," Kavya replied.

"You look lovely today. Don't take that smile off your face. It will heal a wound faster than any other antiseptic in the world," Ratan said, smiling.

Kavya blushed. The way Ratan told her about what he felt looking at her, was pure and directly from his heart, no filter.

Kavya shouted, "Ratan, wait a minute! Can you come back?"

Ratan stopped and walked inside the dressing room.

"Tell me what happened. And before you say anything, I will not make apologies for what I feel about you," Ratan smiled.

"Thanks for whatever you said. I didn't call you about that," Kavya waited.

"I lied to you about Manju."

Ratan squinted his eyes, as if he was confused and said, "What?"

Kavya said, "My mother knew Dr. Manju. But she asked me to stay away from anyone asking about her. And told me that I should tell you that my mother doesn't know anything about her."

Ratan frowned and said, "Thanks for letting me know Kavya. If your mother knows Dr. Manju, then she can help reveal a lot about Manju's past. You won't believe, but there are people's lives at stake now because of Manju."

Kavya looked at him and said, "What can I help you with?"

"It's a long story. If you are free after work here, I can explain in detail somewhere outside. How about over a cup of coffee or tea?" Ratan asked.

Kavya was not sure if going against her mother was something she should do. And why had her mother told her to stay away from anyone asking about Dr. Manju. Once her mother said no to something, it was very hard to work against it. Ratan was looking at Kavya and could understand her dilemma.

So, to convince her, he said, "Kavya, I want you to hear the story first. And if that doesn't convince you to help me, then you are free to walk out. But at least give it a chance and listen to what I want to say."

Kavya thought that there was no harm listening to what Ratan had to say. She was pretty impressed with the way Ratan was communicating his feelings to her.

Kavya replied, "I will be free after 7 pm, but I have to be home before 9 pm."

Ratan looked at the watch. It was 6 pm, so he had to wait for another hour.

He said, "Thanks. I will wait for you outside. And later I will drop you home."

Kavya nodded, and Ratan sat outside in the waiting area.

In House 666/13B, Ravi went to the cupboard and looked closely. He tapped around gently. It smelled of moisture, like old musty furniture. When he tapped on the bottom of the cupboard, there was a hollow sound.

Ravi looked around that board and found a ring hook that could be pulled up. He pulled it out. The plank opened, and he saw a big dark hole with very narrow stairs going down. It was so small that if Ravi attempted to go down, then there was a high chance that he may get stuck. That little passage gave him a feeling of claustrophobia. But it made him realize that it was easy for a slim girl to slip inside the passage and go down the stairs quickly. That was the reason she had vanished from the room in a few minutes.

He bent and looked closely into that dark hole and tried hard to see what was inside. While he was peeping into the pitch black darkness, the smiling face of the girl with red lips and dark circles around her eyes looked at Ravi for a few second and disappeared. He could hear the faint sound of someone running. That sudden appearance of the girl was terrifying. He took quick deep breaths in succession to calm himself down.

He decided to go down into the passage to see what was going on. Ravi barely dared to put his foot in that dark space. But his love for Aditi gave him that push to go inside. The hole was about four-square feet. He looked up, took the name of Lord Shiva, and put one foot forward first. He adjusted himself to fit in that hole and went in. He touched the step with one foot and slowly kept another foot to balance himself. The steps of the staircase were made up of wood. He could feel that the staircase was leaning towards the wall, and it was not fixed because it wobbled at each step he took to come down. The inner wall around the hole was made up of wood and concrete, and it smelled like soil drenched in water, mixed with wet wood and stone. Spider webs covered the walls, but ironically the railing of the staircase was clean.

It meant that someone was using the stairs very frequently. The temperature in that hole gradually dropped, and after a few steps, he started to feel cold. It was pitch dark, but in a few minutes, he could see some light coming from afar. It took him around five to seven minutes to reach the bottom. The base floor was also made up of wood. He could feel that he was not under the ground, but still above it. Once he reached the surface, he felt cold and humid. Around a meter away, there was an electric bulb which was lit. The height of the tunnel was around 4 feet and Ravi had to crawl to move forward. The passage was well ventilated. After crawling around for ten minutes, he reached a door. He pushed the door, and it opened. It opened into a small room about ten by ten feet. Walking through that tunnel and reaching the room felt as if someone had reached a beautiful garden after crossing the maze of a dirt path. There was a bed, a fridge, a washbasin, every essential thing anyone could have in one room. But things were all scattered here and there. As Ravi looked through that window, someone kept a hand on his shoulder. He panicked and jumped back. While doing so, he fell on the floor.

When he looked up, the girl was laughing and giggling at him. This time it was the laugh of a child, carefree and unapologetic. The same girl who had scared the hell out of Ravi was a living human. And this time, Ravi also joined her in chorus.

Looking at Ravi laughing, she stopped suddenly. That was quite strange. It was a complete change.

Ravi also stopped laughing, and holding the bed rail, got up. They both stared at each other.

Tears rolled down her eyes. Ravi was baffled. He spoke softly.

"Hello, my name is Ravi. You scared me upstairs. Who are you?" He extended his hand for a handshake.

She kept looking at him and started to sob slowly.

Ravi was confused. He was trying to figure out what he had done to make her cry. She appeared to be in her teens.

Ravi asked her once again, "What happened? Why are you crying? Is it because I came into your room without your permission?"

Ravi moved towards her, when suddenly his leg got stuck on something on the floor, and he nearly stumbled. The girl began to laugh again and Ravi too joined in. This time the girl kept smiling.

Ravi went near the fridge where he saw a photo frame of a couple and a baby girl. He slowly picked it up and looked at the girl in the picture. He pointed to the baby girl and asked, "Is that you?"

The girl nodded in confirmation.

Ravi smiled and said, "You look so cute here!" He kept the picture back on the fridge.

He asked again, "Where are your father and mother? Why are you staying here in the bunker?"

The girl started to sob again. Ravi felt that he had to make a connection with her so that she would start talking.

Ravi curiously looked around the room while the girl stood quietly on the side. The bloodstains on her dress, the slight blue patches on her face, which had looked terrifying to Ravi a few hours back, now looked more like make-up done for a fancy-dress competition at the school. There were a lot of unanswered questions in the room.

Ravi said, "See, I need to talk to you. What are you doing in this abandoned house? Talk to me please. What's your name?"

She kept looking at Ravi. Ravi decided that he would start taking a few names so that she may react and say something.

He asked, "Do you know Aditi?"

She shook her head to say no.

"Okay, this house belongs to Manju. Have you heard her name?"

She nodded in the affirmative and pointed to the photo which Ravi held in his hand.

Ravi looked at the picture and asked, "Is this Manju? Is she your mother?"

She said, "Mummy" and started to sob again.

Ravi's heartbeat quickened and he asked, "Who are you? Hema?"

She tapped herself on the chest and said, "Me, Hema."

Ravi couldn't believe that he was looking at Hema. He had heard from Aditi that Hema had left the house with Ajay. How was she here?

Ravi asked again, "Where is your mother, Hema?"

She stammered and said softly, "She comes here sometimes."

That answer shocked Ravi. Manju was alive! He sat on the bed and covered his face with his hands. He once again picked up a picture and asked, "You are this girl Hema, and she is your mother, Manju?"

She nodded and smiled.

Ravi continued, "And your mother is with you?"

She smiled again and nodded.

Ravi had come into the house looking for an answer about Aditi, but instead, he had uncovered the truth about Hema and Manju. Ravi decided that he had to know the details about both Manju and Hema and why they were hiding. He put her hand on Hema's shoulder.

"Hema, I am happy to see you here. But why are you hiding here? I need to find an answer. I want to meet your mother. When will your mother come?"

Hema said, "In the night she comes. Brings food."

Ravi couldn't wait anymore. He had to go out and tell Ratan about what he had uncovered. They could both come down here and try to meet Manju.

He said to Hema, "Hema, I have to go now. But surely, I will be back. I can't let you stay here much longer. It's a crime. You need to see the world outside. And above all, why has Manju dressed you like this?" Ravi walked towards the staircase.

Hema pulled Ravi's hand and took him to the other side of the room. After walking for a few moments, they came across a staircase.

Hema pointed and said, "Go here, go."

Ratan thanked her and walked up the stairs.

The staircase led to a storeroom. He looked around. Furniture was scattered everywhere, and he could smell the dampness in the air. He looked for a way to exit that room, and he found a staircase going up. He took the stairs, which led him to the main hall on the ground floor. Ravi came out through the main door and reached the scooter.

A voice said to him, "Bye bye!"

This time he ignored the voice and carried on.

He turned back and looked at the house. It looked gloomy and terrifying. It was as if the house was looking at Ravi and telling him that it had a collection of many unknown facts, yet to be discovered.

Ratan was waiting for Kavya in the lobby. A little after 7 pm, she walked out of the room and looked at Ratan in the waiting area. Kavya gestured that she would change her dress and meet him in the parking area. After a few minutes, Kavya came out wearing a salwar kurta. Ratan looked at her, and his eyes followed her till she reached him.

Ratan requested Kavya to go to a coffee shop nearby, instead of the one in the hospital. He would be more comfortable talking to Kavya, and she would also be able to listen to him without being observed by hospital staff. Just a few minutes, drive from the hospital, they reached a coffee shop. They both sat down. Ratan told Kavya about Ragini and Manju. He kept talking for the next half an hour. When he had finished his story, he convinced Kavya to find out more about Manju from her mother. Kavya listened to Ratan and agreed to help him. For Ratan, this was a double bonus – he would not only get more information about Manju, but would also get another chance to meet Kavya. On the coffee table, they both exchanged phone numbers. Kavya promised to let Ratan know if she found anything about Manju.

Ratan said, "You don't know how grateful I am. Ravi is more than my brother; I am doing all this for him. And Aditi, she is a poor girl. I am sure we will find something which can help both."

"Don't worry, Ratan. I will try my best. I know my mother is a tough nut to crack, but I will somehow manage to get this information from her." Kavya smiled.

Ratan looked at her, and that smile of hers was more intoxicating than any drug.

"Come, I will drop you," Ratan said.

"I think you should go and take rest, Ratan. In this condition, you should not be driving," Kavya said, looking at his head.

"I don't want to miss the opportunity to drop you back home. As I said before, your smile can treat any wound. Come, hop on!" Ratan insisted.

When Ratan was coming back after dropping Kavya, his phone rang. He stopped his bike on the side and picked up the phone,

"Hi Ravi, tell me."

Ravi said, "Where are you? I am at your home."

"What happened? What are you doing there?" Ratan asked.

"I can't tell you everything over the phone. I went to that house," Ravi said.

"Which house?" Ratan asked.

"That house, the one where we went with Aditi. You come. I will tell you what I found there," Ravi said.

"Okay, I will be there in the next thirty minutes. Stay there," Ratan said.

Ratan reached his house and saw Ravi walking around his room, anxiously.

Ratan looked at Ravi and asked, "I know what you will say."

"What will I say?" Ravi frowned.

"That you saw Aditi there," Ratan said.

"What?" Ravi exclaimed in surprise.

12
Friends Forever

Ravi looked at Ratan with disappointment and said, "What are you saying? Why are you always bringing up Aditi?"

"I am sorry, really sorry. I was kidding. Tell me what you saw there?" Ratan said, pacifying Ravi.

"Ratan, I am serious. Please, don't bring Aditi between us always," Ravi said in frustration.

"Okay, I got it. Here, I have zipped my mouth about her. Now please tell me what you saw in the house?" Ratan asked.

"Manju is alive, and I met her daughter Hema in the house," Ravi said.

"What?" Ratan said in shock and continued. "Ravi, please. Now I said I am not going to ask about Aditi. Please, you don't kid with me. It's not the right time," Ratan replied.

"Ratan, I am serious. I met Hema there in the house. She said Manju is also there in the house," Ravi said.

Ratan thought that it had something to do with Aditi. It might be her trap for Ravi.

So, Ratan went near Ravi and said, "I think you should not go in that house, Ravi."

"Why?" Ravi asked.

"See, I am not sure what you have seen inside the house. It might be true also. Or it might be something paranormal. You know that house is haunted," Ratan said.

Ravi laughed at that and said, "Ratan, Ratan, Ratan. I, too, believed that there was a ghost inside. But no, they are human like us."

"And where did you see them? When we went into the house, there was no one, right?" Ratan said in a commanding voice.

"Yeah. But you remember that voice in the room and the voice while coming out of that house. What was that? It was Hema. She wanted to scare us," Ravi said.

"Why? And Hema is with Ajay, right? Based on what that girl said," Ratan replied.

"That girl? That girl's name is Aditi," Ravi stared at Ratan, and then went on.

"And, I am not sure what exactly happened in the house. But Hema is there in that house. "

"Okay, did you tell this to Aditi?" Ratan asked.

"No, not yet. But why?"

"See, I have found out something about her," Ratan said and suddenly stopped.

"Enough!" Ravi said in a loud voice.

"I am telling you about Hema and Manju. And you keep on bringing up Aditi," Ravi said in an angry voice.

"Ravi, think again. Manju is dead," Ratan said, looked at him for a second.

"Why would she be in that house? And if she is there, why doesn't she live a normal life in that house?" Ratan asked.

"We can ask Manju this," Ravi said.

"And have you seen her?" Ratan asked.

"No, but Hema told me she comes at night," Ravi said.

"Ravi, I think you should stay away from..." Ratan said and stopped suddenly.

"From?" Ravi asked.

"I want you to open the G.B. photo shop and look after the shop," Ratan said to Ravi.

"So that I can stay away from Aditi?" Ravi said sceptically.

"Tell you what? You take some rest. The accident has had a severe effect on your brain. I will take care of myself and do what I have to do," Ravi said and started to walk out of the Ratan's room.

Ratan kept one hand his on his shoulder, pulled Ravi hard to stop him.

"Ravi, wait, listen to me!"

Ravi shrugged off his hand and shouted at him.

"I can't leave her alone in that distress, Ratan. This is not going to work. Since the beginning, you have not wanted me to stay with her. And you are now levelling absurd allegations about that poor girl. Enough of it, Ratan. I never thought that a girl coming in my life would change you so much. Goodbye!" and he was walked out of his room.

Ratan saw him go and said to himself, "I will never change for you, Ravi. I will find out the truth behind Aditi, and then you will realize how much I care for you."

Here Ajay had decided to leave the city forever. Before leaving, he decided to go to Manju's house as he didn't want to live the rest of his life with Manju's memories. He reached the house where he thought he would never come back. He reached the door and looked at the façade of the house. Glancing through the house he said, "Manju, god gave us life and we decide whether we make it good or bad. Sometimes I think I shouldn't have got involved. But what could I have done! I didn't want to lose you. You came into my life, you supported me, but then you ditched me. You left me. I will be leaving this city forever. I am moving on Manju, but it doesn't mean I don't love you, but now I don't want to carry this pain anymore. Bye!"

When Ajay turned back, he heard something near the window. He saw a girl dressed in white, blood stains all over her face. He looked closely and murmured, "Hema?"

The girl looked at Ajay and screamed as if she has seen some ghost and ran inside the house. Ajay laughed like a maniac. He had been waiting for this day, for so many years. She was actually inside Manju's house. Hema was finally found. He decided that he would go back and bring all the things required for the rituals. He would follow the steps of Akalkhand in Manju's house. He swiftly ran towards his bike and decided to get everything back quickly. He was pumped up, as his hunt was finally going to end.

It was hard for Ratan to convince Ravi about Aditi's condition. He knew Ravi was in love with Aditi, and when a man is in love, he is like a child – easily elated or dejected. Ravi didn't want to lose Aditi, which was why he could not see her on the wrong side of the fence.

Ratan thought of leaving Ravi alone and speaking to him in a day or two when he was in a better frame of mind. That should be enough to think about what Ratan had said to Ravi. And Ratan too was not ready to accept the reality that Ravi had met Hema in the house.

After two days, Aditi got the report of her MRI scan, and to her surprise, there was nothing in it. Sometimes finding nothing can also be cause of worry when you have already made up your mind on an outcome, expecting it not to be in your favour. Aditi had thought that her report would reveal why she had been behaving differently for the last few months. But her MRI report was clean. But she knew that mentally she was not the same Aditi.

She got a brief from the doctor over the phone, and the doctor wanted to have a detailed discussion with her in the hospital. Aditi texted the same message to Ravi. She told Ravi that she would go by herself and pick up the report as the doctor wanted to talk to her. That day, Aditi felt lost.

She went into Dr. Ketan's room, where the doctor had her results.

Dr. Ketan looked at Aditi and said, "Aditi, the good news is all is normal. There is nothing to worry.

"See Aditi. I know you were expecting that this report would tell you the cause of problems which you have been facing lately."

Dr. Ketan showed Aditi a small line on her MRI result, the top left side of the circular image of the brain and asked her.

"Did you meet with an accident a few years back? This has nothing to do with your vertigo problem or anything else. I am just asking as this line stands out in the image."

Aditi looked at it and remained quiet. Dr. Ketan could see a tear rolling down from her eyes. He felt that Aditi had been reminded of a past trauma.

He said, "It is fine, Aditi. If you don't want to tell me, it's okay. Please have some water."

Aditi kept looking at it.

Then suddenly she shouted, "No, no, stop. Leave me!"

Dr. Ketan was stunned. Few nurses and ward boys standing outside of his cabin came rushing inside.

Dr. Ketan looked at the nurses and ward boys and signalled to them that they should wait outside. Dr. Ketan stood there and waited for Aditi to calm down. After a few minutes, Aditi sat on the chair and wiped her tears.

The doctor gave her a glass of water and said, "There is nothing in the report, Aditi. You are fit and fine. Take some rest, and I will call you if required."

The doctor smiled and escorted Aditi outside the cabin.

Aditi came out of the doctor's cabin as a girl who kept running away from her past, so much so that she had even left the city. That memory which was in front of her, that fateful night had changed Aditi's life forever.

Dr. Ketan knew there was something from her past that was haunting Aditi. Whatever it was, she was trying hard to suppress that memory. He also knew that if it remained engraved in her mind, it could amplify in the future. She needed to replace this part of her memory with some good ones. It's like replacing the land of cactus with a lush beautiful garden, full of flowers.

He checked in the system if there were any relatives of Aditi listed so that he could check with them about Aditi's past. He found Ravi's number there and called him. He told Ravi that he must come alone and to not let Aditi know that he was meeting the doctor.

Ravi hung up the phone and said to himself, "Why does everyone want to meet me about Aditi and also that I should not tell her about it? That day it was Dr. Parichit, and now Dr. Ketan. Strange! I can't let her suffer all this; I need to talk to her about it."

After a couple of hours, Ravi reached the hospital on his scooter to meet the doctor.

Dr. Ketan explained to Ravi what he had experienced with Aditi. "See Ravi, I told you everything. A doctor never shares anything about his patient with others without the patient's consent. But this case is different; the way she reacted is unusual and sad. She had lost her parents some time back. So

I need someone close to her to talk to her. I saw your phone number, and I hope you are close enough to take care of her," Dr. Ketan looked at him.

Ravi was listening to him with his head down.

He nodded his head and said, "Just like you asked me not to tell Aditi about this, someone else also told me his experience with Aditi, and he also asked me not to let her know about me meeting with him."

Dr. Ketan frowned, "Who?"

Ravi said, "Dr. Parichit. Do you know him?"

Dr. Ketan knew that Dr. Parichit was the guru of parapsychology sciences. If he has experienced something worth the worry, then it should be a severe case, and it may have a different angle to it.

He said to Ravi, "Who doesn't know Dr. Parichit! He usually visits our hospital for special cases. I am not sure what he saw, but if he is saying something which may be a cause for worry, then you must seriously think about it and talk to him."

Ravi said, "You know what? When I met Dr. Parichit in the hospital, he told me that you can wait for the MRI report but you won't find anything. I didn't believe him that day, but it looks like he was right. "

There was complete silence in the room.

Then the doctor asked Ravi, "Did Aditi tell you anything about her past? Something which she doesn't want to remember or something that happened in her life which changed her completely?"

Ravi gave a thought and said, "One day when we were having lunch, she did tell me that she was an orphan as she had lost both her parents in an accident, and she didn't want to remember her past. But it was all normal talk. It was indeed an unfortunate incident, but she told me about that incident very casually."

The doctor said, "See Ravi, Aditi is running away from her past. She's trying to suppress her memories, but that is not the correct way to handle it. If you have a bad incident in your life, you have to replace that with a beautiful one. I think this is one reason she keeps herself busy at work, but that is not a solution. Someone has to make her life beautiful so that she forgets what had happened to her before."

Ravi replied, "But why does everyone keep telling me that I should not talk to her about meeting with them. Earlier it was Dr. Parichit, and now you."

Dr. Ketan smiled and said, "The sole reason is that we want you to heal her wounds, not aggravate the situation by telling her about the injury itself. You can surely tell her that you met us, but when the time is right. Right now, she needs to be handled gently. Stay with her."

Ravi received a text message on his phone and looked at Dr. Ketan,

"It's Aditi. She wants to meet me."

Dr. Ketan said, "Here you go. God has chosen you for a purpose; to solve Aditi's problems. Take care of her."

Ravi nodded his head. "One thing, doctor, what if she speaks about what happened with her. Will that take the burden off her shoulders? Will that help her in some way?"

Dr. Ketan said, "Yes, surely, but I can't say what would be the right time to ask her that. Or let her tell you herself when the time is right."

Ravi thanked him and walked out of the cabin.

He was in deep pain because it had been almost three days since Ravi had spoken to Ratan. It had never happened before between them.

Ratan was lying down on his bed, thinking of how to help Ravi and Aditi. His phone rang, and he saw Kavya calling. He looked at her name, and his heart started to pump a little faster. He picked up the phone.

Kavya told Ratan about Manju and what her mother knew about her.

"See, Manju was an expert surgeon. She was pretty famous, and even today, some doctors in Gangaram Hospital refer to her research papers. During their stay in Gangaram Hospital, something happened. Doctors say she was in deep love with Ajay. Things started taking a wrong turn when she was caught stealing a patient's non-functional organ. My mother said it was a kidney. It was Manju's belief that burring that organ in the cremation ground would help treat a dying person's kidney. People say that she did this because Ajay influenced her to do that. One theory says it was her deep love for Ajay that made her do this. Others say that she herself initiated this to get some kind of kick. One day a doctor observed that a patient who had died after Manju operated on her, had precise cuts on their body. In the mortuary, organs were missing from dead bodies. It is just that she was one of the best surgeons in Gangaram Hospital and they needed her.

"Then one day, god knows what happened and she married the trustee Ramchandani. And a couple of years later, she was found dead in the house. Doctors or nurses believe that since she was doing all these occult practices, her body had suddenly vanished from the mortuary. The only thing I can say is that Ajay is still alive and Manju's daughter Hema too. I think you can get more information from Ajay. Rumours are going around in Gangaram Hospital that Ajay is in town. Someone saw him in the city, in some clinic. They say he received a neck injury in an accident."

Ratan said, "Can we get Ajay's picture from somewhere?"

Kavya replied, "That one is easy. When my mother told me the story about Manju, she showed me a couple of pictures where Dr. Manju and Dr. Ajay were standing close to each other. I will get it for you."

Ratan said, "Thanks Kavya. You have done a lot for me. Somehow I need to hunt down Ajay, and then he can tell us the true story."

"I will send you the picture on your phone," Kavya said.

Ratan promptly asked, "How about meeting over a cup of coffee?"

Kavya paused and those few seconds were like hours for Ratan.

"Okay, when do you want to meet?"

"Tomorrow, same time, same place."

Kavya agreed, and Ratan could feel that mushy feeling in his heart. He realized that a simple word like 'yes' or 'okay' could change a person's mood, like rain in the dusty, dry, and hot desert.

The next day, Ratan met Kavya in the café. He reached the café a few minutes earlier and waited for her. Kavya arrived a little later. Kavya gave the picture to Ratan and pointed to Ajay. Ratan could recognize Manju as he already had a photo of her. Ratan took a screenshot of the picture which Kavya had brought.

Ratan and Kavya talked over coffee. They talked a lot. Both were enjoying each other's company and were opening up to each other. Ratan was falling in love with her. Kavya, too, reciprocated his sentiments.

Ratan drove to Kavya's house. It was late at night, but she was not bothered at all. Ratan had found something beautiful while uncovering the truth about that gloomy house.

Ratan reached his house, carrying the memory of the blissful moments he had spent with Kavya. He wanted to be in that dream world the whole night.

A mile away, Ravi suddenly started to feel alone. The only place he thought could be away from Ratan and Aditi was Saleem uncle's stall. He rode his scooter and sat there, alone in the corner. Someone tapped his shoulder. He was startled and looked behind to see Saleem uncle.

"What happened, boy? Where is the other guy?" he chuckled.

Ravi said without any expression on his face, "He might be at his home."

"What happened? You look quite serious? Did you complete the job?" Saleem uncle asked.

"The job," Ravi chuckled sarcastically and said, "It's not a job but has become a joke."

"I have never seen you this serious. Ratan was the one who always plays that part. So, tell me, what happened? Let me give it a try and see if I can solve some of your issues," Saleem uncle said.

"Leave it, uncle! It's a long story, and I want to stay alone to find some solution to it," Ravi said dejectedly.

"Why is Ratan not with you?" Saleem uncle asked.

"He doesn't necessarily need to be with me always," Ravi said.

"You guys fought?" Saleem uncle asked. Ravi didn't respond to that question.

"Let me call Ratan here and talk to him," Saleem uncle said and took out the phone from his pocket.

Ravi held his hand and said, "Don't call him uncle. He won't come. He met with an accident a few days back."

"Oh! When did this happen?" Saleem uncle asked.

"Couple of days back," Ravi said.

"When you were with Aditi? That night?" Saleem uncle asked.

"Yeah, that same night," Ravi said.

"I had warned him. He went to that house alone," Saleem uncle said.

"What?" Ravi was shocked to hear that and continued, "What did you say uncle?"

Suddenly, it struck Saleem that Ratan had made him promise that he should not tell this to Ravi.

"Nothing, Ravi nothing," Saleem uncle said.

Ravi looked at Saleem uncle and said, "Uncle everything around me has become a mystery. No one is responding to me with a proper answer. Why? Even you. You know something, and you don't want to tell me. Looks like there is no place in this world left where I will get some answers. It was difficult and now getting even worse," Ravi said and stood up.

"Where are you going?" Saleem uncle asked.

"I don't know," Ravi said and walked away from there.

Ravi drove the scooter back to his home. While he was going in the lane near his house, he saw the same guy, Ajay, whom he had hit that day. Ajay was sitting inside a tea shop. Ravi looked at him and parked his scooter outside the shop, and slowly went inside. Without letting Ajay know, he sat very quietly beside him.

Ravi looked at him.

"I am sorry, that day I hit you very hard. I know it's late, but I am really sorry about what happened," Ravi said.

Ajay was shocked by that sudden voice and looked at Ravi. As soon as he saw Ravi sitting beside him, he started to scoot, but Ravi held his hand.

"Please sit here uncle. I won't do anything to you. There is nothing good happening in my life. At least a 'sorry' to you will make me feel better. How is your neck, by the way?"

Ajay sat there without speaking a word. Ravi insisted, and after some effort, Ajay told him.

"I visited a doctor. There is some problem in the cervical nerves C1 and C2. It will be fine after physiotherapy and medicine."

"Where, which nerve? C1? It looks like you know the issue in detail," Ravi said.

"I am a doctor, retired. I don't practice now," Ajay said and started to walk out.

Ravi didn't say anything. As he saw Ajay get up from the seat and walk to the exit, he suddenly blurted, "My name is Ravi Bhagat. What's yours?"

He replied, "Ajay" and went on his motorbike.

Ravi shouted, "Sorry for that day. I think it's never too late to make things right."

Ravi smiled, and drove back home. Apologizing to Ajay had made him feel lighter, as if a load had been taken off his chest. Ravi decided that the best thing he could do was speak to Dr. Parichit about Aditi.

The next day he called up Dr. Parichit's number. His Personal Assistant (P.A.) picked up the phone and Ravi introduced himself.

The P.A. replied, "Dr. Parichit has been waiting for your call. Right now, he is not in the office. Once he is back, I will let him know that you had called. Leave your phone number with me."

Dr. Parichit's P.A. took the phone number from Ravi before hanging up.

Ratan got a call from Chhote Maharaj. He told Ratan that Sadhu Maharaj wanted to speak to him. Ratan had never thought that he would receive a call so soon. Sadhu Maharaj came on the phone and said, "Before I tell you anything, answer a few questions. Listen to them very carefully and tell me what you remember correctly. Only what you have seen. No assumptions. Your answer should be correct and should explain to me how it happened. Don't bring any greed or bias in your response. Can you do that?"

Ratan was slightly nervous. But he was ready for whatever questions Sadhu Maharaj had.

"Yes, Maharaj, I will tell you whatever I have seen."

Sadhu Maharaj paused and asked few questions regarding Aditi. Ratan was calm and slow in his response, fearful that he may say things which he might not have seen. Ratan also spoke about his meeting with Ragini and narrated all that he had heard from her.

"When you saw her in that house, did you feel something strange? Something that an average human can't do?" Sadhu Maharaj asked.

Ratan told him about the incident of how he had got hit by the table. He had thought that Sadhu Maharaj would be astonished, but his reaction was neutral. One of the reasons could be that he didn't want Ratan to get influenced by his response.

Sadhu Maharaj waited for a few seconds and said, "Aditi is possessed, and the person who is inside her is dominant on Aditi. As of now she is safe; it means that demonic power only comes when it feels it is being challenged by someone less powerful, like a normal human. But once the work of the demonic entity is over, she will take total control of her, and Aditi will be gone forever. You have to find out what her goal is. What is she seeking in the afterlife? If she is Manju, we need to find out what has been left incomplete in Manju's life. You need to stay alert and keep all you loved ones alert too. I will have to meet Aditi in person. I will be in town tomorrow. If you want her to be safe, then I need to see her in person. Can you do it?" Sadhu Maharaj asked.

Ratan knew it was very difficult to convince Aditi to meet Sadhu Maharaj at such short notice. The only person who could make it happen was Ravi.

He said, "It's difficult, Sadhu Maharaj. But I will try."

"One more thing, Ratan, tomorrow is Amavasya. The power of demons will be at the peak during this time. Stay alert," Sadhu Maharaj said and told Ratan to keep chanting the mantra which Chhote Maharaj had given.

Ratan hung up and sat on the chair. He was wondering how he would arrange a meeting between Aditi and Sadhu Maharaj. It was impossible. He picked up the phone, dialled Ravi's number, and then cancelled the call. The scene where Ravi left the room, not wanting to hear a word against Aditi, flashed before his eyes.

Ravi saw Ratan's missed call. Breaking up is easy but fixing things back is the most difficult task.

At that moment, the only person he wanted to speak to was Aditi. Ravi sent her an SMS,

"Are you at home or in office?" and waited for a reply.

Just in a couple of minutes, he got a response,

"Home."

Smiling, he got on his scooter and drove towards Aditi's home.

A couple of kilometers away from Ravi, it clicked Ratan that he had noted Aditi's number once when he was in her office. He thought of meeting Aditi and gauge if she would be agreeable to meeting Chhote Maharaj. Although this was difficult, there was no harm in taking chances. He took out the phone and called her up.

"Hello Aditi"

"Yeah, who is this?" Aditi asked

"It's Ratan here," Ratan said.

"Is it possible to meet you somewhere?" Ratan asked.

"What happened? Is everything okay?" Aditi asked.

"Yes, everything is good. And yes, we are doing your job. Don't worry about it," Ratan replied.

"See Ratan; I can't come anywhere. And I am not feeling well too. If you like, you can drop by my home," Aditi said.

"Okay, how about now? Is it okay with you?" Ratan asked.

"Yeah, it's okay. I am here," Aditi said.

"Address?"

"Yes, I will WhatsApp you my address and location," Aditi replied.

"Thanks Aditi. Also, please I have one request, don't let Ravi know about me coming down there," Ratan spoke up.

Aditi agreed and hung up the phone. Just after a few minutes, he saw a message forwarded by her. Ratan dressed up and went to Aditi's home.

This was the first time Ratan was meeting Aditi after that incident. He was praying that Manju should not surface in Aditi while he was there. He needed to watch out that he should not offend the spirit inside Aditi in any way, else it would be a difficult situation to control. The security guard at Aditi's building asked him for his details. Ratan wrote down all the details.

Aditi's flat was just near the elevator. He came out of the elevator, walked a few steps and knocked on the door. Aditi opened the door and looked at Ratan.

Ratan almost closed his eyes; he started to feel the sweat in his palms.

She chuckled and said, "Why are your eyes closed? Come in!"

Ratan opened his eyes, gave a forced smile, and walked behind her inside the house.

Aditi cleared some space for him on the sofa and asked, "Feel comfortable. Do you want some coffee or tea?"

"Nothing, I am fine. A glass of water, please," Ratan said.

Aditi bought a glass of water and extended her hand to give it to Ratan. She looked at Ratan and asked, "What happened to your forehead? Where did you get this so badly?"

In that house, Ratan was alone with Aditi. He was preparing himself mentally that anything could happen anytime. The spiked heartbeat never settled down and the unusual cold in the room was making him uncomfortable. He had read somewhere that a sudden drop in temperature indicated the presence of spirits. He was not getting any positive feelings sitting there.

Ratan stammered, "I fell from my bike. The doctor says it will be fine in a couple of weeks. I am okay now."

"That must be quite painful, right?" Aditi asked. She was rubbing her forehead as if she had a headache.

"How are you? Are you feeling okay? Looks like a migraine," Ratan asked.

"Yeah, I don't know what's happening to me. Migraine, vertigo, sometimes telescopic vision. I did some checkups, but nothing came out." Aditi replied as if she was in deep pain.

"Tell me, why are you here?"

"I want a small help from you. I want you to meet one person; he will be in town soon." Ratan asked her in a soft voice.

"Why do you want me to meet him?" Aditi asked curiously.

"He has something to share with you. Just listen to him. He might also have some cure for your issue too," Ratan said with his hands cold.

"Why will he have a cure for my issues? I mean, who is he?" Aditi leaned backward and looked up at the ceiling.

"This headache is worsening. I can't even see the ceiling properly! God knows what is happening to me."

"His name is Sadhu Eknath Maharaj," Ratan said.

Aditi went quiet. Ratan looked at her. Aditi had leaned backward completely on her couch, in a sitting position. She was looking upwards towards the ceiling. With both her hand on her thighs, her legs were slightly spread.

Ratan waited for a few minutes. He thought she had drifted off to sleep.

After waiting for a few minutes, Ratan asked, "Aditi? Are you okay?"

She moved her head to face Ratan, eyes closed, and murmured slowly.

"Sadhu, Sadhu, Sadhu, Sadhu." She kept repeating, and her voice slowly transformed from thin, soft-spoken to thick and growling.

Aditi was sitting on the sofa, eyes closed, legs spread, hands on thighs, and her lips constantly moved to repeat those words. Her lips were stretched enough to show how annoyed she was with that name, "Sadhu."

It sent a chill down Ratan's spine. He had awakened Manju inside Aditi.

On the way to Aditi's house, Ravi went to a flower shop. He looked around and picked a few, got confused and then kept them back. He asked the staff to help him after he had exhausted all the options. Finally, he found a bouquet that he felt Aditi might like He kept it in the front basket of his scooter and drove towards Aditi's house.

Ratan was stunned to see what Aditi had turned into. One thing he noticed was that she had a severe headache, after which things turned south. Ratan had seen how powerful Aditi could be. He was cautious and put his hands on his head to prevent a new injury.

Aditi looked at Ratan with eyes closed and giggled in a strange voice, "You you you, there there there. You are alive. Alive alive alive."

Ratan said in a shaky voice, almost shivering voice, "Manju, I know you are there inside Aditi."

Aditi giggled "No, no, no. Aditi is inside me. My slave slave, slave," and she suddenly stopped laughing and talking.

Aditi slowly started to come down from the sofa, kept both the hands and legs on the ground. She began to walk towards Ratan like an animal on four legs. Eyes closed, no expression, moving straight towards Ratan.

She came close to him. Ratan was frozen to the spot.

Aditi looked at Ratan. She was so close to Ratan that he could feel the warm air on his chin and neck when Aditi was breathing out. Then Aditi opened her eyes. The eyeballs were still and not moving at all. Ratan was numb and didn't even realize that Aditi had kept her hand on him.

His eyes pleaded to her. Ratan asked, "Aditi? Are you listening to me?"

Aditi's eyes swiftly turned, and with her mouth wide open, she said, "Let her sleep."

Ratan said, "I can help you, Manju. Tell me, why are you here?"

She laughed in a ghostly voice and said, "Aditi is here inside me. I am here to protect her. Both of them need me."

"Protect her from whom? And who both?"

"Those greedy, insane, humans."

"Who are those humans Manju? I can help, we all can help whoever you want to protect."

"You all are the same. Everyone is the same. You kill everyone who loves you the most. I will kill you all," Aditi said in a growling voice.

"And what about Hema? Do you know where Hema is?"

Aditi looked at him again with soulful, pleading eyes, and then squinting, she shouted in a growling voice, "You can't find her. She is safe, away from all of you." And she smashed a thick book on Ratan's face, and he fell instantly.

"Manju, I am here to help. Tell me why are you doing this to Aditi?"

"You want Sadhu Eknath to meet Aditi so that I leave her. It won't happen. They can't take me away from Aditi," Aditi growled and continued. "I won't let this happen." Aditi jumped and sat on Ratan's chest, grabbing his neck with both hands and choking him.

Ratan tried to remove her hands. The strength in Aditi was enormous, and Ratan started to suffocate. He tried to grab whatever came in the vicinity of his hand and hit Aditi with it on her back and then on her head. It was a small ceramic pot that was kept on the table, and had fallen off on the floor when Aditi had jumped on Ratan.

Aditi touched her head, and there were small traces of blood in her hand. Ratan pushed her aside, and Aditi's hand was off from his neck. Ratan started to breathe again. Aditi jumped back towards him, and in walked Ravi. Aditi looked at Ravi and immediately fainted.

Ravi looked at Aditi and was shocked; there was blood coming out from her head. Ravi looked at Ratan.

Ravi shouted at Ratan, "What the hell were you doing?"

Ratan got up holding his neck, and coughing he said, "Listen to me, Ravi."

"Don't come near me, Ratan. Else, I won't be able to control myself," Ravi said in an angry voice and rushed to Aditi.

Ratan went near Ravi and yelled, "Enough! You have to listen to me Ravi. After that, whatever you want to do, I am okay with it. But first, take Aditi to a hospital."

Ravi looked at Ratan, didn't say a word, and searched for the car keys. Ratan looked at Ravi and how he was moving inside the house, as if he had been there earlier. Ravi finally found the keys. He and Ratan carried Aditi to the car for the hospital.

The doctor immediately took her to the operation theater to put stitches on her wound.

Ratan and Ravi sat outside. It was time for Ratan to tell Ravi what had happened so far.

Ratan went near Ravi and said, "Remember Ravi, when we were in class 8 and everyone who had not done the homework was getting punished by the teacher? Those were brutal ten strokes of bamboo stick on our hands. You didn't complete the assignment too. I told you, Ravi look into your notebook; I know you have done it. You didn't believe me because you knew you didn't complete it. I kept on telling you to look into your notebook first, but you never listened to me. Then when the teacher asked, you said that you didn't complete the work. And I shouted that you have done the job, took out the notebook from your bag and showed it to the teacher. You got saved from those ten brutal strokes. That day, I did your homework before the class started when you were busy impressing that girl in the class."

Ratan chuckled, but Ravi was silently listening to what Ratan was saying. Ratan looked at him and held his hand.

He sat on the ground near him and said, "Today also, I was trying to save you from the same pain. Believe me, Ravi. I didn't know how strong your love was towards Aditi. But for me, your friendship is the strongest bond I have ever treasured. No one can break this. What I did is to save you first, and then Aditi."

Ravi looked at Ratan. His eyes were wet. That was enough to believe Ratan.

He asked in a pained voice, "Then what was that... I saw in Aditi's house?"

Ratan smiled and said, "Let me tell you what I was hiding from you for a couple of days."

He sat on the chair and narrated all that had happened to Ravi. This time Ratan didn't hide anything that might later raise any suspicion between them.

Ravi was stunned.

Ravi got up and hugged Ratan tight.

Ravi said with wet eyes, "You don't have to be sorry, Ratan. You have all the right to do what is best for me. Even I can't take that right away from you. This is meant to be forever. A forever friendship."

They hugged again, this time, even tighter.

13
What goes around comes around

Ratan said, "Now what? Sadhu Maharaj is coming tomorrow to meet Aditi. And I think Aditi should meet him."

Ravi replied, "Before that, we need to speak to someone."

"Who?" Ratan asked curiously.

"A parapsychologist, Dr. Parichit," Ravi said.

"Who is he?" Ratan asked.

"He was the first one amongst us to have identified that Aditi has issues related to the paranormal or a split personality. He tried to convince me but I kind of shrugged it off, "Ravi said.

Thinking about what should be done next, he took out the card that Dr. Parichit gave him. The secretary immediately connected him to Dr. Parichit.

"Is everything okay Ravi? How is Aditi?"

Ravi told Dr. Parichit all that had happened with Ratan, and that they were at the hospital where Aditi was admitted.

"It has become more prominent now. You stay there in the hospital. I will come there. Make sure you don't trigger her in any way. Once the dominant other comes up in front of all of us, then it will be hard to bring Aditi back. Wait there, I am coming right away," Dr. Parichit said and hung up the phone.

Ravi and Ratan waited for Dr. Parichit to come, and to meet Aditi in his presence.

After a few minutes, the doctor came out of the operation theater. It was not a critical operation, but they wanted to keep Aditi in the hospital for at least two days.

Ratan and Ravi agreed to what the doctor said. While they were talking to the doctor, the nurse wheeled Aditi out on the stretcher. Aditi was in deep sleep; the oxygen mask was on, and saline water dripped through. Ratan looked at Ravi. He did not want Ravi to feel more depressed in this situation.

Ratan tapped his shoulder and said, "She will be fine, Ravi. Stay strong."

They waited at the hospital for Dr. Parichit. Around one hour later, Dr. Parichit came. He was in the same attire, in a grey shawl and three broad white lines drawn on the forehead, with a red dot of vermilion in the center.

Ratan looked at him and said, "If I didn't know this was Dr. Parichit and he were to walk by me, I would never know that he is a doctor."

"The same thing happened to me when I first met him. He is a genius, a guru," Ravi said in a reverential voice.

Ratan said, "Why do brilliant and geeky people behave so differently? Lucky we are not that brainy!"

Ravi grinned and said, "Shut up!"

"Where is she?" Dr. Parichit came near both of them and asked about Aditi.

Ratan pointed and said, "Room number 1212."

Dr. Parichit told them his thoughts.

"Right now, Aditi may have become weak because of the wound, but the other personality inside her might still want to use all the strength left in Aditi."

"Manju, her name is Manju," Ratan said.

"Manju who?" Dr. Parichit asked.

"Aditi is possessed by Manju," Ratan said swiftly.

"She is not possessed. In parapsychology science, this is called a split personality disorder. People generally confuse it with demonic possession," Dr. Parichit said with a calm, smiling face.

"Let me go in and see her. I will see her from afar. Ravi, you go in near her. Ratan, you stay with me," Dr. Parichit instructed.

They both nodded their heads and agreed to what Dr. Parichit said. Ravi walked towards the room, and Dr. Parichit and Ratan followed him.

They reached the room silently. Ravi looked at Dr. Parichit. He waved his hand to say, go in.

Ravi opened the door; the bed was empty. Aditi was not on the bed.

Ravi asked in loud voice, "Aditi?"

Dr. Parichit asked, "What happened?"

"She is not on the bed, Dr. Parichit," Ravi said, worried.

Ratan and Dr. Parichit looked at each other and exclaimed,

"Not there? Where did she go?"

Ratan rushed to a passing nurse and asked, "Sister, do you know where Aditi is?"

"Aditi? Who?" the nurse asked.

"She was just brought out from the OT and shifted to this room," Ravi yelled.

The nurse walked inside the room and checked the clipboard hanging near the bed. The name of the patient had been scratched out.

She said, "It so weird, she scratched out her own name," and briskly walked out of the room and called other hospital staff using the intercom.

Within a few minutes, three-four staff gathered. One of them was a ward boy who had shifted Aditi to the room.

He said, "I shifted her inside the room. She was given a Pentazocine injection for deep sleep, so she should be asleep for at least 5-6 hours. But it's shocking to see that she is not here. Where would she have gone?"

Aditi was gone from the hospital.

It was a tense situation for the hospital. One patient had gone missing, and none of the staff had noticed. They all went to the security monitoring room, looked at the lobby cameras, and focused the camera at the room. What they saw shocked them to the core.

Just twenty minutes after Aditi was shifted into the room, the room's door opened. Aditi walked out of the room like a normal person, dressed in the light blue hospital gown. She was moving so briskly that the scene shocked the staff. They had never seen a patient walking so comfortably after being operated on and given a dose of Pentazocine injection. Every face in the monitoring room had a terrified look as if they had seen something unusual like a ghost or spirit walking out of the room. The only person who looked unmoved was Dr. Parichit. When Ratan and Ravi saw Dr. Parichit, they were amazed to see him slightly smiling in that terrifying situation. Now, the big question was, where had she gone.

Dr. Parichit said, "See I told you. The other one will use everything in her capacity to take over Aditi. Poor girl!"

The first assumption was that she had gone to her own house. Aditi's house. Ratan and Ravi quickly moved out of the room; Dr. Parichit looked at them. He asked where they were going. When they told him of their plan of going to Aditi's house, Dr. Parichit told them something strange.

"The person you just saw is not Aditi, it is Manju. And Manju will not go to Adit's house."

"So, where will Manju go?" Ravi asked curiously.

"To her own house," Dr. Parichit replied.

"Oh god! She might have gone to meet Hema," Ravi said.

"We need to go there," Ratan said.

"No, we can't go there now without knowing what exactly Manju wants. Right now, Manju has taken control of Aditi's body. If we try to put pressure on her, she might harm people around her and herself. And we will lose Aditi forever," Dr. Parichit said, with a worried expression.

"What Manju wants, only one person can tell us now. That is Ajay. He is in town, but searching for him is like finding a needle in the haystack," Ratan said in frustration and sat down on the chair.

While they were thinking what to do, Ratan took out his phone and opened the image gallery to see Ajay's picture.

Looking at him, he said, "Where are you? For god's sake, come out."

Ravi went near him and asked him to show the picture. He took the phone from Ratan and looked at the image. He glanced at it and gave the phone back.

"That is a familiar face. I know I have seen him somewhere. But can't remember exactly where," he thought aloud.

Ratan looked at Ravi said, "You have seen Ajay?"

Ravi repeated, "Ajay, Ajay, yeah Ajay," and then he shouted.

"Ratan, this is Ajay."

Ratan frowned and said, "Yeah, indeed it is Ajay."

"No Ratan, this is Ajay. Ajay," Ravi said in excitement.

"What happened to you, Ravi? Are you okay?" Ratan asked him.

"Of course, I am okay. I know where we can find Ajay. You remember a few days back I had hit a guy while he was wearing the helmet, and hurt my hand? That was Ajay," Ravi said.

"What? How do you know he is Ajay?" Ratan asked, surprised.

"That's a long story. I know where he will be now," Ravi said.

Dr. Parichit said, "See, whatever we have to do, it should be swift. There are a lot of things that we have to do in a short time. What does Manju want? What does Ajay know?"

"What if we bring Ajay in front of Manju? If there is something that Manju wants to tell Ajay, she can do it then. That would be the quickest way!" Ravi said.

"Ajay's life will be at risk. But who will bring Ajay to the house? What will you tell him?" Dr. Parichit asked.

"You leave that to us. Tell me doctor, will this help?" Ratan asked.

"Yeah, it will help. But Manju will either leave forever or she might stay forever. It depends on what Ajay knows about Manju. And how good he is at convincing Manju to leave," Dr. Parichit said.

"Let's bring Ajay and take him to the house,"Ratan said.

"You guys bring him to the villa. I will wait for you outside the villa, and then we all will go in," Dr. Parichit replied.

"Sounds like a plan," Ravi said.

Ravi shared the address of the house with Dr. Parichit and went with Ratan to find Ajay.

Ratan got a phone call, "Son, I am in the town. Can I meet Aditi today?" Chhote Maharaj said to Ratan.

Ratan kept his hand on his face as he didn't have an answer to that.

He said, "Chhote Maharaj. We are in quite a situation here," and Ratan explained what had happened in the hospital while they were going to bring Ajay.

"So, Sadhu Maharaj, we are going to the same house in the hope of finding Aditi there. I will send you the house location. See if you can come there," Ratan said and hung up the phone.

After a thirty minute drive, they reached the tea stall near Ravi's house and waited for Ajay.

Ravi saw Ajay on his bike, going out. Ravi looked at him and nudged Ratan,

"Here is our Mr. Ajay. But where is he going? Let's go, let's go!"

They both sat on the bike and began the chase.

He was carrying a large bag on his back, riding through the lane on his motorbike. Ravi wondered what could be inside the bag. They kept on following him, hoping that he would soon stop, so that they could convince or force him to come along.

Ratan noticed that Ajay was taking the route to the villa. He tapped Ravi and said, "Did you see, he is on the same route which goes to Manju's house? He is making our job easier!"

After a long chase, Ajay reached Manju's house. Ajay got down from the motorbike, and held the bag. The way he was handling it, it seemed very heavy. He took that bag and went inside the house. Ajay was in a hurry, he didn't want to lose Hema now. He reached the door and swiftly went inside. Ajay went in and started to clean the floor surface. After cleaning it, he took out a jar of salt and drew a big circle. Then he took out the book of Akalkhand and started to flip the pages. After flipping to the last page, he stopped and kept the book open in front of him and started chanting one mantra. One after another, in the next half an hour, he created a circle overlapping the salt which was colored with red and white. He took out a big urn, kissed it, and kept it at one side. Next, he took out the surgical kit, which included gloves, a knife, and cotton. This terrified Ratan and Ravi.

While they were looking at all this through the window, Ratan's phone buzzed. Chhote Maharaj told Ratan that he would arrive at the place very soon. Ravi and Ratan were baffled now. On one hand, Ajay was about to begin a strange ritual and on the other hand, Dr. Parichit and Sadhu Maharaj were reaching there.

Ajay got up from the place and went into the rooms upstairs, to search for Hema. While Ravi and Ratan were looking through the window, Aditi walkout from the inside of the room into the hall. She was wearing the blue hospital gown and was very tired. She felt as if all the strength had drained out from her. She walked slowly and stood near the circle. She went near the urn, looked at it and smiled. Within a moment, that smiling face turned angry. Dr. Parichit came and stood behind Ratan and Ravi near the window.

He tapped their shoulders and whispered, "Look at her, it's a typical case of multiple personality disorder, a split personality. Aditi is Manju now. We have to be careful, very careful. You make one mistake and we will lose Aditi. She will be gone forever."

While Aditi was looking at the circle, Ajay came from inside looking around, walking into the hall, empty handed.

He looked at Aditi and shouted, "Who are you?"

Aditi slowly lifted her head, smiled, looked at Ajay and said, "Many years back, when you were here, you blew that Strychnine (a toxic powder) and left us to die. That killed me and Ram. But now I am back." She paused and asked, "How are you Ajay? Looks like you have lost something."

Ajay was looking at Aditi with surprise and asked, "Who are you? And how do you know about Manju and Ram?"

"I am the one whom you loved. I am the one whom you killed," Aditi said angrily.

"Rubbish! What are you talking about? Who are you?" Ajay repeated in shock.

"I am Manju!" Aditi growled.

Ajay was shocked when he heard that name.

"Manju? That's not possible. Akalkhand says, you cannot take a new body unless…" and Ajay stopped.

"Unless you take out Hema's heart," Manju shouted.

That voice was so terrifying that everyone was stunned.

Ajay now knew that he was looking at a body possessed by Manju. He swiftly went to the Akalkhand and started to chant mantras.

Aditi walked towards him but Ajay pushed her away with all his strength. Aditi fell down, hit the floor head first, and became unconscious. Hearing the sound, Hema came up shouting,

"Mumma!" and ran towards Aditi.

Ravi said, "Hema thinks that Aditi is her mother?"

Dr. Parichit said, "Hema has seen Manju. Unless Hema has some psychological issues, it can't be possible."

Ajay looked at Hema coming out and said with a smile, "My prize, my heart." He paused and said, "Manju, now soon you will be born again. Only for me." Ajay held Hema by her arm and threw her on the floor.

Ratan shouted, "You monster!" and ran inside the house.

Ajay looked at Ratan and following him, Ravi and Dr. Parichit also ran into the hall. By this time Ajay's hand was inside his bag. He quietly took something in his hand and blew the stuff over all three of them. Ajay smiled.

"Time to sleep, boys!" he said.

It didn't take much time for all three to fall down and become unconscious. Whatever Ajay wanted to do, he had to do it quickly. They would be conscious very soon. He tied up Hema's hand and legs and put her inside the circle. Then he took out one injection of Propofol and injected Hema so that she goes in deep sleep. Hema was in deep sleep within minutes.

He looked at her and said, "Everything is set. We have a patient, who is going to die soon and an audience to witness this miracle or rebirth." And Ajay laughed out loud.

He got up and tied up all of them – Ratan, Ravi, Dr. Parichit and Aditi too, so that they wouldn't cause any hindrance in the ritual he was going to perform.

Ajay looked up and said, "Kaal, please accept my sacrifice. Please bring my Manju back. With this offering, you will be obliged to fulfill my wish. Here I bring her heart at your feet."

And he took out the surgical knife and started to make a cut on Hema's chest.

"Lord Shiva is more powerful than your Kaal. Ajay! That's why we all call him Mahakaal," Sadhu Eknath Maharaj walked into the room shouting and chanting Lord Shiva's name.

Ajay wondered what was happening all of a sudden. But this time, it won't be that easy to tame Sadhu Eknath.

"Don't challenge my Kaal, Eknath. I know you very well. You have been defeated in the past by the tantric and now it's my turn," Ajay shouted,

The sadhu was shocked as to how Ajay knew that he was once defeated by the tantric. That made Sadhu Eknath realize that this time, the beast was bigger. Sadhu Eknath walked towards Ajay chanting the *shivstotram,* but someone pulled him back holding his hand.

Aditi walked out from behind Sadhu Eknath and grabbed Ajay's neck, holding him high, his feet up in air, and shouted, "Before even fighting with Mahakaal, you need to defeat a mother."

Aditi threw him a few feet away on the floor.

Sadhu Eknath Maharaj took out some water from his bag, and chanted mantras holding the water in his hand.

Here Ratan was waking up from the effect of the powder that Ajay had thrown at him. He found himself tied up with a thick rope. He looked around and found Ravi and Dr. Parichit sleeping. Both of them were tied up as well. Ratan dragged himself towards Ravi and shook him. Slowly, Ravi also woke up. They looked at Hema on the floor. Aditi was standing in front of Ajay, who was also on the floor looking at her. And Sadhu Eknath Maharaj was chanting mantras.

Ratan said, "Sadhu Maharaj!"

Ravi said, "Hema in that circle?"

Both echoed, "What's going on?"

Aditi swiftly picked up the copper urn and threw it on Ajay's head. Ajay tried to dodge, but it hit him on the shoulder. That hit was so painful that he sat holding his shoulder and screamed in pain.

Sadhu Eknath saw that and realized that Manju would not leave Ajay alive.

He held Aditi's hand and said, "Don't kill him Manju. Else, if you go to jail who will look after Hema?"

Aditi shook her body to free herself from Sadhu Eknath. Sadhu Eknath realized that Aditi was using all her strength now. There was blood all over her face. Sadhu Eknath untied Ratan, Ravi and Dr. Parichit. Then he quickly moved Hema out from that circle and moved her aside.

Ratan went towards Ajay, held him tight while Ravi rushed with the rope.

Dr. Parichit held Aditi, grabbing her around her waist, and said, "Manju, you have to go. Let Aditi take care of Hema. You have suffered enough in this world. I promise Aditi will be a fantastic mother to Hema."

Ajay was forced to sit on the sofa, and Aditi stood looking at him like a statue. Dr. Parichit knew that Manju would not leave her unless she had taken revenge from Ajay.

Sadhu Eknath went close to Dr. Parichit and said, "She is still in there. She has not left Aditi yet."

Dr. Parichit squinted and loosened the grip on Aditi. In that very moment, Aditi ran towards the circle, picked up the surgical knife, came back and sliced it through Ajay's neck. That cut was small in size, but was exactly on the spot where the vein connection flows to the brain. It could only be Manju who knew how to make that cut. A stream of blood came out from Ajay's neck and splashed on Aditi. He started shaking as if a high voltage current was passing through him.

Sadhu Eknath said to Dr. Parichit, "Thank you, doctor."

Dr. Parichit said, "I understand Sadhu Maharaj. There was no other way to save Aditi. At least a monster is dead."

Ratan and Ravi were standing there, without moving. What they had seen was so terrifying that it was a shock for them. Aditi fainted in front of Ajay, and the floor was covered with blood all around. Her blue hospital gown was slowly soaking up the blood coming out of Ajay's body. Manju had left Aditi forever.

The news of what had happened in Manju's house had spread like wildfire. Ravi and Ratan were all over the newspapers.

People called them by many names – ghostbusters, paranormal investigators, or spirit hunters.

Few days later

Ratan and Ravi went to meet Aditi in the hospital. Ravi went closer to Aditi and she said, "I am sorry that you had to go through all this."

"Whatever I have done, I have done for you Aditi. But now, see you have a purpose in your life – Hema. I know you will take care of her very well," Ravi smiled.

"Hema was always my purpose to live. It was my greed that I took her away from the mental hospital long time back, without letting Ragini know about it. But now, it's better for all of us that we all three – me, Hema and Ragini – live together," Aditi smiled.

Ravi continued, "I think, I have to go back and look after GB studio. Promise me Aditi, we will be friends forever. If you need any help, anywhere, remember, I am just a phone call away."

Ratan said, "I have one question Aditi. How do you know so much about Manju?"

"Leave it Ratan, let's not bring it up," Ravi said promptly.

Aditi pulled out a diary from the table and handed it over to Ratan and said, "That day when I went with Ragini in that house, I got this diary. Manju used to write a diary entry daily. She has written every moment of her life."

Ratan smiled and flipped through the pages of it. And Aditi continued,

"Please keep that with you Ratan. I don't need it now." She smiled.

Few weeks later

Ravi received a phone call from Aditi. She was leaving this city forever with Hema and Ragini.

Ratan looked at Ravi, and asked, "I can't imagine that you didn't propose to Aditi!"

Ravi smiled and replied, "I still love her, and there is no doubt about it. But I don't think she feels the same way about me. So, it's okay to let her go. At least, that didn't break my heart."

"Does the heart also have bones?" Ratan asked and both guffawed.

While they were laughing about it, a short, fat guy walked into GB photo studio and asked, "Are you guys, Ratan and Ravi?"

"Yes, we are the owners of GB photo shop. Do you want photographers for a wedding shoot or birthday parties, function or any event?" Ravi said.

The guy kept quiet and took out his mobile and showed them a video clip. In that clip a girl was talking to a mirror, there was no voice, and astonishingly they couldn't see her reflection in the mirror. After a few seconds, she took out a knife and slashed her wrist. Blood spurted out. It was a very shocking and disturbing scene. The girl was laughing, looking at the mirror.

The guy paused the video and said, "Don't worry, she is alive. It is not the first time that she has done this to herself. She is my daughter."

He pulled out a cheque book, and hand over a signed blank cheque to Ratan.

"I have heard a lot about you guys. You both have solved the mystery of Dr. Manju. Please I beg you, save my daughter!

Write any amount on this cheque, take the money. Just save my daughter, please!"

Ravi looked at Ratan. Ratan looked at Ravi and shook his head.

Ravi looked at the man and asked, "First, we will listen to your story... that will tell us more about your daughter. Then we will think about it. How about we listen to your story over a pav bhaji?"

Ratan and Ravi looked at the man, and he said, "Sure!"